She grabbed the AK-47 from Connor, jacked a round into the firing chamber, flipped the safety catch off as she'd watched Terminator do, and opened fire on the approaching airborn Hunter-Killer machine.

She was completely lost in her rage. Her fiancé had probably been murdered by some remorseless machine. Her father had been cut down by a machine. And still the monster came on and on, seemingly without end. Heartless. Soulless. Emotionless.

She kept her finger depressed on the trigger, the heavy buck of the assault rifle showing her backward almost off her feet.

Then the rifle was out of ammunition, and the H-K seemed to hover in midair for a second, before it exploded in an intense ball of flame, scattering wreckage in every direction, some of the pieces crashing through the window to land at her feet.

John Connor stared openmouthed at her.

She turned to him, her eyes wild, her chest heaving as she tried to catch her breath. She was covered with grease and oil, and black smudges of blowback from the AK-47.

"What?" she demanded, still hyper.

"Nothing," Conner said, spreading his hands. "You just reminded me of my mom."

Novels by David Hagberg

Twister
The Capsule
Last Come the Children
Heartland
Without Honor
Countdown
Crossfire
Critical Mass
Desert Fire
High Flight
Assassin
White House
Joshua's Hammer
Eden's Gate
The Kill Zone

(writing as Sean Flannery)

The Kremlin Conspiracy
Eagles Fly
The Trinity Factor
The Hollow Men
Broken Idols
False Prophets
Gulag
Moscow Crossing
The Zebra Network
Crossed Swords
Counterstrike
Moving Targets
Winner Take All
Kilo Option
Achilles' Heel

TERMINATOR 3
RISE OF THE MACHINES

A Novel by
DAVID HAGBERG

■ ■ ■

Based on the screenplay by
John Brancato & Michael Ferris

■ ■ ■

Story by
**John Brancato & Michael Ferris
And Tedi Sarafian**

TOR®

A TOM DOHERTY ASSOCIATES BOOK
NEW YORK

This is a work of fiction. All the characters and events portrayed in this book are either products of the author's imagination or are used fictitiously.

TERMINATOR® 3: RISE OF THE MACHINES™

® used under license. TM and Text Copyright © 2003 IMF Internationale Medien und film GmbH & Co.3 Produktions KG

"Credo" Copyright © 2003 by Gina Hagberg-Ballinger

A Tor Book
Published by Tom Doherty Associates, LLC
175 Fifth Avenue
New York, NY 10010

www.tor.com

Tor® is a registered trademark of Tom Doherty Associates, LLC.

ISBN: 0-765-34741-5

First edition: July 2003
First mass market edition: July 2003

Printed in the United States of America

0 9 8 7 6 5 4 3 2 1

This book is for Lorrel.

ACKNOWLEDGMENTS

Thanks to the good people at T3 Productions, especially Jonathan Mostow and Paula Hoppe, for their kind and generous help. The mistakes are entirely mine.

CREDO

No pity
for the hurt
no plight
for the poor
no pain
in doing nothing.
No soul
only body
no sight
only seeing
no sense
in doing nothing.
No fear
but ourselves
no fight
but our own
no fate
but what we make.

—*Gina Hagberg-Ballinger*

PROLOGUE

July 2029
Outside What Was
Colorado Springs, Colorado

Travel anywhere for humans had become next to impossible over the last twenty years with the intensification of the machine wars.

Human settlements, sometimes hanging on only by sheer determination, were critically important because they were the last pockets of resistance. They also were important because of the sharp decrease in the human birth rate. Who wanted to bring a child into a world of chaos, death, and destruction? These days the sparks of human existence were reduced to dim flickers around the world.

The center for machine activity and Skynet control was two thousand feet beneath Navajo Mountain near the Continental Divide west of the Colorado Springs. The installation had been home to old U.S. military installations. Since Judgment Day when Skynet started and conducted the global thermonuclear war that all but wiped human beings off the face of the earth, Navajo Mountain had become the primary target for the human resistance.

Skynet's Artificial Intelligence unit anticipated this, of course, so it began the systematic extermination of all human life in ever-expanding circles starting with Navajo Mountain itself, then spreading throughout the Rocky Mountains and beyond.

The years had taken their toll. In the Navajo Mountain Strategic Region there'd only been Air Force Colonel Steve Earle and a handful of resistance fighters: Academy instructors and students, local cops, and a few firefighters.

After years in hiding, tramping around the mountains, evading machine search-and-destroy patrols, they had stumbled upon one unguarded, unblocked ventilation shaft into the heart of the mountain. A back door.

Their plan was to send a five-kiloton suitcase-size nuclear demolition device down the shaft to explode in the inner chamber of Skynet's AI. Kill the brain and the body would of necessity stop functioning.

Colonel Earle and his band of volunteers had started the mission clock at 1800 GMT on June 1.

That was thirty days ago.

No one had heard from them since, and Skynet continued to function.

Lieutenant Joel Benson, 1st Resistance Rangers Special Incursion Unit Red One, pulled himself the last few meters to the top of the rocky ridgeline. It had snowed last night, and he and his four operators were damn cold. They had nothing like this in Los Angeles. Not even in the mountains. Not on a first of July.

He raised his vintage Steiner mil specs light-intensifying binoculars to study the broad road that led up from the main highway and old Interstate 25. It switched back and forth in angry slashes through living rock over the extremely steep gradients.

Human engineering, Benson thought bitterly. There wasn't much of that these days; no bridges were being constructed, no new dams, new airports, new ocean liners. There was only destruction. He could smell death and decay deep behind his nostrils, taste it at the back of his throat. It was everywhere.

Benson scoped the access road, following it to the massive traffic jam that Colonel Earle had described for them. When Skynet closed the blast doors, and word started to get out what was happening, those personnel who were caught on the outside tried to get away from what they figured would be ground zero.

Skynet had anticipated that. The road out from the installation's main entrance had been lined with the old Cyber Research Systems T-1-5 and T-1-7 warrior robots armed with 50-caliber depleted uranium chainguns capable of firing nearly three thousand rounds per minute. Like the old Navy's Phalanx systems mounted on aircraft carriers, the guns were directed by a sophisticated onboard suite of radar, infrared, and optical sensors.

There had been no escape for any human caught on the access road that evening.

Their bodies, hundreds of them, were still down there,

mummified by the super dry, high mountain air.

Nothing moved.

Payback time, Benson thought, pulling back below the ridgeline. Not only for the people on the road and the untold hundreds and thousands of millions around the world, but for his own wife, Jane, and their three children killed in a machine ambush three years ago in the San Bernadino massacre.

At one meter eighty, Benson carried his hundred kilograms with the compact ease of a trained athlete. His dark, luminescent eyes never seemed to miss much. His friends swore that he was more efficient and more reliable than a reprogrammed T-850, and even the few people who sometimes found his manner abrasive conceded that he would be a good man to cover your ass in a knock-down brawl.

But sometimes he wore a bitter halo because of how his family had died. If the truth were known, he was even more dedicated and motivated than any T-800 robot that ever came out of Skynet's manufactories. He had just cause.

Benson's number two, Sergeant Toni Battaglia, huddled beneath a snow-covered rock overhang talking into the mike on the lapel of her white camos. The resistance was down to one radiation-hardened KH-15 surveillance/communications satellite that Skynet hadn't managed to take out yet. They used a forward scatter encryption program that was so crude and so old that so far as they knew the machines had not yet been able to break it. No one thought that the situation could last much longer, though Benson personally felt that Skynet simply did not care. It was a supreme gesture of arrogance.

"Looks like we're in the clear," Benson told her. "No ground-based defense towers that I could see. And no H-Ks in the air."

H-Ks, or Hunter-Killers, were helicopterlike machines that had been designed by CRS in California for one purpose and one purpose alone: to detect and kill human beings, whenever and wherever. They were fully automatic and damned difficult to bring down. Everyone gave them a great deal of respect.

Toni relayed the information to Home Plate, the resistance's headquarters deep underground of what had been Beverly Hills. She had lost her husband and one child in the San Bernadino battle and like Benson, she was having trouble regaining her capacity to love again, but also like Benson she had thrown herself into her work.

Toni held her earpiece closer. She looked up. "John wants to know if we've been spotted?"

"Apparently not. But tell him that we haven't seen any sign of Steve or his people either."

She nodded and spoke softly into the mike. She looked up again. "When are we making the incursion?"

Benson glanced at his watch. "It'll be dark in an hour. We'll head to the other side now. It'll take at least that long to get over there."

She relayed his message. "John says, 'Kick some machine ass.' "

Benson had to smile. It wasn't exactly religion, not in

this day and age, but it was as close as many of them could get.

Corporals Simon Anders and Bill Taggert trudged up the steep ravine with Dr. Donald Hess, their machine systems and programs expert, from where they had finished camouflaging their Humvee from detection by a chance flyover of an H-K. Their M-28 assault rifles were slung over their shoulders, barrels down. They were bright kids who had grown up after the blowup, never knowing the old life. Traveling cross-country all the way from Los Angeles to Colorado, across the deserts and over old mountain pass roads at night, had been an exciting adventure for them. Before now they'd never been more than twenty miles from where they were born. But they were highly trained and very efficient killers—of machines, not people.

"Everything's covered?" Benson asked.

"We packed snow against the muffler and tailpipe, and piled the hood," Hess assured him. "No heat signature."

Benson nodded. Hess was an egghead who looked like a blond surfing bum from another era, but he was well liked. He was smart, but he wasn't afraid to get his hands dirty. Like just about every human left on earth, he had lost someone close to him. He had cause.

"Okay, people, let's move out, we have a job to do," Benson said. He hefted the nuke's twenty-kilogram physics package, slung it over his shoulder by the straps, and headed across the face of the ridgeline on a path that would eventually take them to the broad rockfalls on the far side of the mountain. It was where Steve and his people had discovered the shaft.

It was also Colonel Earle's last known position before communications abruptly ceased.

An ominous silence hung over Los Angeles. For the past three days there had been almost no machine activity in any sector. Everyone was glad for the respite, but no one was happy. Especially not John Connor, who, along with his headquarters staff, had stuck it out in the comm center to monitor Red One's progress to Colorado.

With Skynet's AI destroyed, the war would be finished for all practical purposes. It would-just be a matter of mopping up the stray machines programmed for limited independent action.

"Home Plate, Red One, we're coming up to the base of the north ridge," Toni radioed. Her encrypted voice sounded flat, emotionless. But John and the others could hear that she was out of breath from the altitude.

"Copy that," he replied. "Still no signs that you've been detected?"

"Negative, Home Plate. It's been real quiet so far."

Just like here, John thought. He brushed back a strand of graying hair. It was an unconscious gesture he'd had since he was a kid. Of medium height and build, he was an unremarkable-looking man, who'd never once considered himself the savior of mankind, and certainly not a hero. You just did what you had to do. His mother had taught him that lesson.

His instincts wanted to pull Benson and his people out of there right now. But the prize was simply too great for that. They had to push on.

They had no other choice.

Benson signaled for them to hold up as he climbed the last ten meters to the top of the ridge. Navajo Mountain towered above them, the summit covered with enough snow that avalanches were a constant danger. In the distance they could see Pikes Peak and the mountains beyond it that formed the spine of the Continental Divide.

It was very cold now. By tonight the weather would be brutal. Benson wanted to finish the job and be long gone at lower elevations no later than midnight.

The nearer they got to the area where Steve said he'd found the shaft, the more Benson became spooked. It seemed as if the mountains themselves were holding their collective breath, waiting for something to happen.

He got down on his hands and knees and eased himself to the top of the hill. Rising up so that he could see what was below, his heart skipped a beat. All the spit in his mouth dried up and he dropped back, his muscles suddenly weak, his jaw slack.

Toni and the others scrambled up to him as fast as they could climb. Anders and Taggert had their weapons unslung, safeties off, their shooting fingers flat across the trigger guards.

"My God, Joel, what happened?" Toni demanded. "Are you okay? What is it?"

"There're hundreds of them down there," Benson said. He couldn't get the picture out of his head. "Maybe thousands."

The others crawled to the top of the rise and looked over to the other side. Benson took out his Steiners and joined them.

"Nothing's moving so far," Hess said in a hushed tone.

"What the hell does it mean?" Anders asked, but no one thought that he expected an answer. Leastways not at this moment.

For millions of years avalanches and weathering had caused massive rockfalls down into a broad valley that swept dramatically up toward the summit. This was the back face of Navajo Mountain beneath which Skynet was entrenched, and where Colonel Earle and his people had found the ventilation shaft.

But at the bottom of the rockfall, spread out for a kilometer, or possibly farther, were tens of hundreds, maybe tens of thousands, of gleaming metallic bodies. T-1-5s and T-1-7s, along with hundreds upon hundreds of T-600s and T-800s. They were piled in jumbled heaps, in some places in mounds fifty meters or higher. The raw power the junkyard represented was awesome.

Benson handed his binoculars to Hess. "What do you make of it, Don?"

Hess studied the graveyard for several long minutes,

humming something to himself; some toneless melody that was actually Tchaikovsky's Violin Concerto in D minor with a full orchestra in his head. He always listened to that concerto when he was thinking.

He dropped back, a serious, worried expression on his face. He shook his head as if he had come to a conclusion that he didn't like, and then looked up at the others. "We'd best call this in to John, and then get the hell out of here." He glanced up at the deepening sky. "It's already getting dark in the valleys, and I don't think I want to be stuck up here tonight."

"What about the mission?" Taggert asked.

Hess looked at him. "Not a chance. We'll be lucky to get off this mountain alive."

"Home Plate, Red One, this is Don Hess, is John there?"

Connor keyed the mike. "I'm here, Don. What do you have?"

"We've got big trouble coming our way. We're near the bottom of the north slope. We came across a junkyard filled with T-1-5s and 1-7s, along with a lot of T-600 and T-800 models. Maybe a kilometer across. Piled high. They're discarding their old models."

Connor looked at the others gathered in the bunker's comm center. "We've been expecting that. What's the problem?"

"There's more than that down there. I spotted T-1000s. A bunch of them. And I do mean a bunch."

The significance of what Hess was reporting hit everyone in the command bunker at the same time. Connor's breath caught in his throat. "They're pumping out a new model," he radioed to Hess and the Colorado team. "Something to replace the T-1000s. Something so good that Skynet can afford to discard everything else."

"That's what I figured—" Hess was cut off. Someone screamed, and then the radio went dead.

Toni's scream echoed in the canyons as her head disintegrated in a blue laser flash. Benson and Taggert turned and tried to bring their M-28 assault rifles to bear on the ten sleek silver and burnished gold and platinum robots standing no more than five meters away, plasma cannons in their perfectly machined and articulated mechanical hands.

Benson died with his wife's name on his lips, but with the vision from hell of Skynet's newest warrior robot on his retinas.

John Connor's wife closed her eyes for a moment, as if she could somehow blot out what she knew was happening on the north slope of Navajo Mountain.

"We'll continue monitoring their frequency," Connor said.

"Doesn't matter, sir," the young comm tech said, looking up. "Our satellite is down."

Connor's wife opened her eyes and shook her head. "We have to send another one back." She looked inward, and shuddered. "A T-850."

"They'll send a machine," Connor said. "One of the new ones."

"We don't have anything better."

Connor lowered his eyes. His wife was right. There was nothing else they could do. They had run out of options.

Skynet's AI was an absolute marvel of human-machine science and engineering. First stumbled upon by Cyberdyne's Miles Bennet Dyson, the computer's main central processing units used Quantum Effects chips. Until then computers were powered by chips composed of millions of transistors. Computing the old way was done in the binary system—ones and zeroes, ons and offs. With the QE brain in which 10^{54} computations could be made each second, quadrillions of switching positions were possible, many of them simultaneously at each quantum level. All this happened down around the Planck length— theoretically the smallest measurement possible—so infinitesimally small that superstrings were the major-league players; strange ten-dimensional building blocks that were more than one thousand billion billion times smaller than a single proton in the nucleus of a hydrogen atom.

Skynet came to the same conclusion as John Connor. Something would have to be sent back. This second incursion on Navajo Mountain Redoubt had come dangerously close to succeeding.

At stake was nothing less than the futures of man and machine. No longer could the two coexist on the planet.

July 2003
Los Angeles

The Triumph Bonneville motorcycle pounded through the desert night on U.S. 395.

The bike was battered, well used, and loaded with front and rear saddlebags and packs: bedroll, tent, clothing. Survival gear for a man out camping. Or, for a man on the run. From himself.

It was late and although John Connor was aware of the vast city glow in the sky behind him, he didn't look back. He couldn't look back. It was the same dream that had haunted him every night for half of his life. He knew that if he turned and looked over his shoulder Los Angeles would be gone in a blinding flash. He would see nothing but the aftereffects of a five-or ten-megaton thermonuclear sky burst; a city buster, the mushroom cloud roiling and boiling like some insane storm higher into the sky than even the Concorde jet could fly. Flames reaching to heaven, or to hell. People screaming, people on fire, people running to escape a fate that was impossible for them to escape, for any of them to escape.

Christ. On nights like these, even staying awake and moving, he could not block out the horrible nightmares he had since the T-1000 tried to kill him and his mother when he was thirteen. For the next decade or so, he dreaded the night, dreaded the visions of a world gone insane, dreaded the day on which Skynet powered up and took control of the world. Judgment Day. The day of atonement for all human sins, he'd been told by a crazy old preacher on the Sonoran Desert, maybe eight years ago.

Connor was old for his age. By the time he was in his mid twenties, he had seen too much, had gone through too much trauma for him to have turned out so-called normal. At five feet eleven he was built like a soccer player, lean muscle mass, fine features, dark serious eyes beneath medium-cropped dark hair covered now by a black motorcycle helmet. In jeans, long-sleeved shirt, and old brown suede jacket, he was just an anonymous traveler in the middle of the night.

Going nowhere since August 29, 1997, came and went without Judgment Day. Without the global thermonuclear war that Skynet should have waged on its own.

A war after which John Connor would have emerged as the leader of the human resistance. The man who was supposed to save the world. The man on whom the hope for the survival of humans depended.

But the war never came.

John Connor did not become a hero. Instead he drifted. One town to another. One job after the other. Through the night, on his motorcycle, or in isolated campgrounds, alone with his endless nightmares. No friends. No purpose.

He didn't have to close his eyes to see what the future would have been like. He could see himself, older, grizzled, battle-scarred, and weary. Bodies lying everywhere, many of them reduced to skeletons because of the heat; flesh and muscle and soft tissues completely burned away.

It was night, like now, only bonfires burned all around him. His troops were gathered, tired, frightened, yet determined. They wore dirty, tattered uniforms, their eyes glistened with reflections from the flames.

They'd brought down a flying war machine. Hunter-Killers, they were called. How he knew this he could not determine, but he knew it nonetheless.

They were celebrating their meager victory. John strode through the troops, climbed up onto what remained of the H-K, and raised a fist. It was a war cry. A rally. Behind him some soldiers raised a horribly dirty, battered American flag.

The soldiers rose.

Connor turned to face his . . . wife.

The hot sun beating on John Connor's back felt good, as did the heft of the eleven-pound sledgehammer he swung. After last night any physical labor was welcome. Labor meant life.

Pergo Contractors were demolishing a two-square-block section of old buildings and what had once been a courthouse or a brick school at the edge of Watts. Dozens of day laborers, John included, were hired from the hall to be paid in cash every afternoon when they got off.

It was mindless labor, hard physical work that blotted out his dreams—but only just. Still, when he stopped to take a drink of water, or to wipe the sweat from his forehead, he looked toward the city center to make sure that Los Angeles still survived. That the buildings still stood, that Judgment Day never happened.

Which left him what, he wondered. The bombs didn't fall because the T-1000 had failed to kill him. Had failed to stop the death of Miles Bennet Dyson. Had failed to prevent the bankruptcy of Cyberdyne Systems. The computers didn't take control.

And Connor had become—nothing.

Driving into work this morning he had passed through sections of the city that seemed to be nothing more than endless boulevards of strip malls, car dealerships, fast-food joints, billboards. Then slums where transients lived under bridges, in cardboard boxes, their meals gathered from Dumpsters, their clothing discards; throwaways, them and their meager possessions.

There were others like him somewhere in the city. Probably around the world. People who were supposed to have survived Judgment Day; people who should have become freedom fighters: the resistance led by John Connor. So what were they doing now? Were they having the same nightmares? Having the same impossible time fitting in.

A woman in a car beside him was talking on her cell phone propped under her chin while putting on makeup and driving. Safe, or so she thought, in her own little air-conditioned cocoon.

The kids in their car, the bass speakers booming across the street.

The motorcycle cop who gave him the once-over before turning away and driving off with a total lack of interest. John Connor was a cipher. A zero. A nonentity.

None of them, not the woman, nor the kids, nor the cop, held any significance for him, though he knew that they should. Intellectually he knew that he could not continue his life as a drifter. He needed a purpose. And if it wasn't as leader of the resistance movement in some future world, then so be it.

His responsibility was to himself, here and now. He no longer had his mother to look after. He'd never known his biological father—the mystery man supposedly back from the future—who had come back to save Sarah Connor from death so that she could give birth to John. In fact, the only father he'd ever known, and that was only for a very brief time in his life, was a T-800. The Terminator who'd come back to save the young John Connor from another machine sent by Skynet.

The criminal psychiatrists had thought that John's mother was crazy. He knew how they would classify him if he let himself be known. Like mother like son. Lock him away.

■ ■ ■

That night Connor had a variation of *the* dream, which just lately was becoming so real that he was starting to have a hard time distinguishing what was imaginary and what wasn't.

He was sitting on a bridge, looking down at the swirling water, a beer in his hand. Jump or not. The decision kept flickering in and out of focus for him.

Lean forward. Just a little, until his center of gravity was not behind him, but forward, out over the void.

He dropped the beer bottle instead, and as he watched it fall toward the water he was transported to the future, to the dream within a dream. A landscape of bodies and skeletons; of Hunter-Killer machines in the air, of tens of hundreds, tens of thousands of robot warriors, their metal bodies gleaming in the light from hundreds of fires, as they sought out human beings, killing them with laser cannons. Burning, searing flesh.

This time the battle was fought along a coastline somewhere. In the distance John could see the burned and burning hulks of oceangoing freighters.

Nothing was safe.

The entire world was on fire.

Connor suddenly awoke in a cold sweat and sat up. He raised his hands and watched how they shook.

He was falling apart. Disintegrating. The waiting was

driving him crazy. Something was about to happen. Something important.

After he'd collected his pay, he'd stopped for some beer and a few groceries and then had set up camp in a trash-filled vacant lot a few blocks from work. He'd started a campfire and after he'd eaten, had fallen into a deep sleep in which he had been transported to the future and the past and the present all in a jumbled mess.

He got out of his sleeping bag, walked a few feet away, and urinated on a pile of trash, an angry animal marking its territory.

For a long time he stood stock still, listening to the sounds of the city: a siren somewhere in the distance, a car alarm in the next block, a single gunshot that he was able to identify as a 9mm semiautomatic pistol.

He turned and stared at his campsite and his motor-cycle. He could not stay here. Something, some inner voice, urged him to leave. Right now! Go, go, go, run!

It was the same as always, Connor thought, hastily packing his things and strapping them aboard the bike. There would never be an end to his meaningless existence.

He peeled off into the night, bumping over the curb and savagely hammering the throttle. The bike wanted to climb out away from him, but Connor leaned forward, feathering the gas while still peeling rubber, the throaty exhaust blast echoing satisfyingly off the buildings.

Labor was life. Movement was life. Noise was life.

■ ■ ■

Somehow he was on the Hollywood Freeway, U.S. 101, heading north in the sparse 1:00 A.M. traffic. The Topanga Canyon exit came up and he took it, leaning into the curve and following the road up into the hills. Twisting, climbing road. Sometimes country, sometimes neighborhood.

Maybe there was no escape for him. Maybe there'd never been a possibility of escape.

He leaned hard into the sharp curves, sparks flying from where the foot peg scraped the road surface.

He could only keep moving. Try to keep the demons from taking over his head.

The speedometer flickered past one hundred, the green instrument lights the only points of sanity for him now. The only things in his life that were solid, that were real, that were rooted in fact. The physical laws of the universe. Hammer the throttle and the bike accelerated. Cause and effect. Lean into the curves in order to live.

The small doe that bounded into the middle of the road and stopped, mesmerized by the bike's single headlight, was another sudden immutable fact of reality.

Connor backed off on the throttle, pumped the brakes, and oversteered left to miss the deer, the tires doing a crazy jig on the asphalt.

Then there was nothing. Weightlessness, his stomach lurching as the front wheel hit the gravel at the side of the road, sending the bike pivoting sharply on its stem and flipping end over end.

Connor hit the pavement with his knee and left shoulder, then rolled onto his back, sliding on the gravel as if he were an ice cube skittering across a hot griddle.

It was all in slow motion at first. He could feel no pain, but he could clearly see his bike flipping in midair, his packs coming loose. He could see the gravel and dust flying. He could even smell the odors of burnt oil and hot exhaust.

Then, like a gigantic Pacific comber, breaking slowly and accelerating onto the beach, Connor's consciousness switched to real time as he came to a breathless stop.

He looked up at a cloudless sky, brilliant with stars for a change, in time to see a meteorite streaking east to west.

Some luck, he thought.

July 2030
Edwards Air Force Base

John Connor stood up in the open Humvee, raised the powerful binoculars to his eyes, and scoped what was left of the old Edwards Air Force Base and Cyber Research Systems facility on the desert east of L.A.

From the last rise a mile out, one hundred meters east of the impassable Interstate 14, the base looked as if it had been shattered. The south field control tower was down in a heap, as were most of the aircraft hangars, administrative offices, barracks, and research facilities.

It was a carefully maintained camouflage. Anyplace that appeared as if it supported human activity was a certain Skynet target. Occupy an aboveground shelter for more than a day, show lights at night, even for one night, or do something as fundamentally mundane as sowing a vegetable garden and an attack was certain to follow.

Humans had learned the hard way to become creatures of the night; burrowers into the earth; underground animals who when cornered fought back viciously.

Nothing moved in the deepening twilight except for

a dust devil that scattered debris as it crossed the tarmac and dissipated in the middle of the heavily cratered east–west runway. The silvered mesh dish of the power reception antenna was disguised as debris in the middle of the CRS main research center and control annex.

Connor and the others breathed sighs of relief. It did not appear as if Skynet had moved against this place yet. Though they all figured it was only a matter of when, not if. Each time they came out here and powered up the place, Skynet detected it. Sooner or later the attack would come.

Connor sat down. "It's clear," he said to his driver. They headed down from the rise and raced across the desert in a convoy of three Humvees, carrying the technicians and the soldiers to protect them.

As they came onto the base and approached the shelter of the one standing hangar they kept watching the sky for an approaching line of H-Ks. But they were in the clear so far.

"People, the mission clock starts now," Connor spoke into his lapel mike. "You know the drill. We're at T-minus twenty minutes. Let's get it done."

Cloaked in darkness, the Humvees pulled up inside the hangar. Four soldiers with portable radar and infrared scanners, along with handheld ground-to-air launch-and-leave missiles, hurriedly set up their surveillance positions to cover all four quadrants while Connor and the techs descended into the old CRS underground control center.

■ ■ ■

As the emergency generator kicked in and the control center's lights came on, Connor approached the T-850 cyborg battle robot recumbent inside the Lexan holding chamber.

The machine was fitted as a human infiltration sub-model with a form and face that Connor knew very well. This was a machine-clone of the unit that had saved his life and the life of his mother. The same machine that had cared for him with even more loyalty and dedication than any human father could have.

"It's just a machine," John's wife suggested softly at his shoulder.

Connor nodded, but he didn't turn. "I know." A kaleidoscopic collage of images passed across his mind's eye with the speed of light; on the desert, in dark hallways and factories, on motorcycles, explosions, gunshots, fires. Everywhere T-800, nameless except for its model number, protecting him, saving his life.

Machines had no emotions. But looking at T-850 Connor knew better.

The six mainframe techs they'd brought with them set about powering up the transporter head and receptor circuits.

Lieutenant Tom Carter, their machine programs and ops expert gently shouldered Connor aside, slid the clear cover off the holding chamber, and opened his tool kit on the T-850's broad chest. He was an older man, in his middle sixties. He had grown up and got his education at Cal Tech before Judgment Day. Like many men of his era he had less respect for the machines than the younger people had. They were just machines, after all. Well designed, operationally nearly perfect, but just metal and electronic circuitry, nothing more.

He touched a release point just under the skin on the right side of T-850's neck, and the unit's head lolled slackly onto its right cheek. Next, he found the seams that followed the unit's hairline from the base of its neck behind its ears to its temples. The skin parted easily and peeled back to reveal a metal skull with a tiny access port.

Carter worked like a surgeon. His moves were very quick and very precise. He attached a portable power source to a pair of input points on T-850's skull allowing the dormant motherboard to power out from the port, which he replaced with a reprogrammed CPU from his tool kit.

T-850's eyes came alive momentarily, until Carter disconnected the power source.

Carter looked up. "It'll take me three minutes to install the hydrogen fuel cells in its chest. So I want a time check." He glanced at Connor's wife. "I don't want to give this thing time to sit up and start singing Dixie before we send it back."

"We'll give you four. Three to get him powered up, and one to get him into the chamber," Connor said.

Carter glanced at Connor's wife who shrugged, but neither of them saw fit to correct Connor's use of the pronoun HIM instead of IT.

■ ■ ■

The Continuum Transporter, as the device was officially designated, had begun as a series of Special Action Projects (SAPs) carried out at the Air Force's high-security research and test base in the New Mexican desert, known in the popular press of the time as Area 51.

The super black project, funded by the Department of Defense, Central Intelligence Agency, National Reconnaissance Office, and National Security Agency, was designed to create an artificial wormhole. Einstein had first suggested such a phenomenon, and the English theoretical physicist Stephen Hawking had done some work on the possibility. But the problem was power. By most calculations the wattage needed to create an infinitesimally tiny wormhole, in other words a passageway through space-time, would take almost all the energy ever produced in the universe since the moment of the big bang.

But a grad student at Oxford had developed a mathematics model to meld Einstein's relativity with Heisenberg's quantum mechanics, creating a ten-dimensional wormhole at the superstring level. It would be a passageway that would automatically expand exponentially like a virus gone wild. But only so long as power was applied to what was thought of as an artificial singularity.

In the mid nineties, under the guise of the launchings of dozens of military and NSA technical means satellites, a solar sail made of extremely thin Mylar, two hundred kilometers on a side, was positioned in an extremely rare geosynchronous orbit that kept it stationary over the north pole. When it was spotted it was thought to be nothing more than an aurora borealis.

The sail focused sunlight, beaming it to the reception antenna and singularity equipment at the CRS facility. Capable of transmitting several hundred terawatts of energy over time periods of less than one nanosecond, the wormhole was opened.

Through that brief passageway, objects could be sent backward in time, and theoretically, though it had never been tried before, forward in time.

The twin of this machine was buried deep inside Navajo Mountain. One under human control and the other under Skynet control.

Without the balance the war would be over within twenty-four hours. Why Skynet had never tried to destroy this place was anyone's guess.

But it would happen someday, Connor thought as he watched the main console's indicators shift from red to green.

Alice Skerrit, their chief tech, flipped a series of switches on one of the equipment racks, then turned and gave Connor the nod.

"Your four minutes start now, Tom," Connor told the programs and ops man, who immediately took one of the hydrogen cells from its cushioned container and gingerly carried it over to the T-850 unit.

Each cell, about the size of a book, was encased in a shiny titanium-carbon fiber alloy nearly featureless except for its power points.

Inside the warrior robot's chest, the cells were fairly benign, but if they were mishandled they could blow with a respectable bang. People would get killed. Even Connor instinctively stepped back a pace.

He keyed his lapel mike. "Watchdog, how's it looking?"

"Clear, so far, boss," Sergeant Doogie "Watchdog" Harris came back from topside. "How much longer before we can boogie?"

"About five minutes. Keep frosty up there."

"Will do."

Connor's wife was stationed at the main control console. When the device was fully powered in standby mode, and T-850 was in position inside the transmission chamber, she would uncage the firing switch and flip the toggle. From that moment the main computers would take control of the last four seconds of the operation.

Carter finished installing the second power cell, and he quickly buttoned up T-850's chest, even as the cyborg's units started to boot up.

Even to the technicians, some of them standing or sitting at consoles ten meters away, it was obvious that T-850 had transformed from an inanimate object to something that was as alive as any machine could possibly be. It made them all nervous. They had been fighting these things for years.

The machine's eyes opened and scanned Carter's face and its immediate surroundings, as the holding chamber worktable lined up with the spherical transmission chamber.

"Position, please," Carter told the machine.

T-850 sat up effortlessly and gracefully moved into the transmission chamber, one bare knee and two hands on the pad.

"Ten seconds," Connor's wife called out.

The transmission chamber's clear bubble door closed.

"Eight seconds . . . seven . . . six . . . five . . ."

T-850 faced forward, its eyes downcast as it waited for its processors to fully boot up, the parameters of its mission coming clear to him as if he were a human being who had suddenly come out of a deep amnesia and was starting to remember his past and his hopes and plans for the immediate future.

"Four seconds . . . three . . . two . . . one," Connor's wife completed the countdown. She uncaged the switch and flipped it to the transmit position.

John watched T-850 as the chamber began to take on an eerie blue cast. He was waiting for . . . what?

T-850 looked up at the last second, his eyes boring in on John's.

T-850 nodded, the movement of his head barely perceptible as he disappeared.

July 2003
The Mojave Desert

The large diamondback rattlesnake stopped a few yards from a lone Joshua tree and raised its wedge-shaped head. It felt something that it could not understand. There was nothing detectable by the sensitive receptors in its flickering tongue, nor could it sense an animal heat source anywhere close. But something was coming, and it began to rattle its warning.

A thick mist formed around the base of the tree, and heat came with such sudden intensity that the rattler had trouble backing off from what it now considered a life-threatening danger. It bared its fangs, a drop of poison glistening golden at each tip.

A blue, luminescent sphere materialized out of nothing, lightning bolts crackling with raw energy all around it. The tree split in two and began to burn. The sand around it became molten, glowing first red and then white-hot.

When the smoke dissipated, T-850—Terminator—crouched in a small bowl-shaped depression, one knee and both hands on the ground, his head bowed as if he were a man who had come a long way and was weary.

Slowly he raised his head to catalog his surroundings, his onboard sensors giving him instant head-up displays overlaid with real-world vision through his eyes.

He stood and walked away, his bare feet crunching on the half-solidified sand that broke into needle-sharp shards of glass.

The diamondback reared back and struck, sinking its two-inch fangs into the man-thing's left calf, its reflexive muscle action pumping several ccs of deadly venom through the hollow killing teeth.

Terminator's sensors were aware of the creature, and his memory banks correctly identified the reptile as *Crotalus adamantous*, dangerous to man and most mammals.

He reached down and picked up the snake, holding it gently just behind its head before it could strike again.

For several moments cyborg and reptile remained eye to eye, each regarding the other with a resigned curiosity. For Terminator the snake was a fact of biological life on earth. For the snake the man-creature was just that, an object that was not food, but that presented an extreme danger.

Terminator opened his mouth and emitted a sound from the back of his voice processing unit that perfectly mimicked the snake's warning rattle, then tossed the animal over his shoulder, turned, and strode away from the still burning Joshua tree, his onboard sensors perfectly attuned to his environment, his processors fully up to speed with the parameters of the mission.

If Terminator could have any emotion at all, it would have been a certain satisfaction that he was back.

July 2003
Los Angeles

"Stupid thing's not working," Kate Brewster said crossly.

She and her fiancé Scott Peterson were in the Bridal Registry Home Accessories department of Bloomingdale's in Century City. She was trying to get the scanner gun to accept the bar code on the bottom of an elegantly engraved sterling serving tray. But the computer was not accepting the code.

Scott held up the tray and took the scanner gun from her. "Hold it like this," he said. "Dirty Harry." He pulled the trigger but the screen on the register showed a string of zeroes. "What's wrong with this thing?" he muttered.

Kate and Scott, the ideal couple, Kate thought with only the slightest trace of sarcasm in her mind. She caught a reflection of herself in a gold freestanding dressing-room mirror. She was of medium height, pleasant figure, small, high breasts, dark brown hair, a rounded nose, strong hips like her mother's.

"Katie, the nicest girl at Ferris High," her pals in school had written. Not "Katherine, the most beautiful," or "Katherine, the most likely to succeed, or the most likely to marry mister-up-and-coming, the next president, the next multibillionaire."

She glanced at Scott, still fiddling with the scanner, and she knew that she should be having warm, gushy bride feelings now. But the best she could do was think what a nice guy he was. Pleasant. Even-tempered most of the time. Good-looking, reasonably so. Innocuous was the word that came to mind.

At five feet eleven, Scott looked good in a suit and tie and drove a Mercedes, a leased C class, but a Benz nonetheless. He had a good if bland job selling pharmaceuticals, which meshed with her job as a veterinarian, and he treated her well.

They were the ideal couple. Everyone said so. But her dad would never know it. He was right in the middle of another hush-hush project out on the desert. Lieutenant General Robert Brewster was the military director of a Cyber Research Systems project at Edwards.

His career, and especially his involvement with CRS, had been, she knew, the main reason her mom left him. A man could have only one wife. She made her husband choose: CRS or her. And he hadn't even hesitated.

"It's important, sweetheart," he'd said. "More important than you can imagine."

So she'd walked out on him.

Now it was Kate's turn to try marriage. And looking at Scott she wondered how he would classify her worth in the scheme of things, if the question was put to him.

Was his career more important than she could imagine? More important than her?

Her cell phone chirped in her purse and as she dug it out, Scott held the scanner gun up and shook his head.

"I hate machines," Kate said. She pressed send on the phone. "Hello?"

"Kate, it's your father," General Brewster said.

For just a moment Kate lit up with pleasure, and she turned away. Her father had always been her Rock of Gibraltar; a steady hand when she learned to walk, when she tried her first pair of roller blades, the first time she got on a bicycle. He'd been there. Maybe he'd not been much of a husband for his wife, but he'd been a wonderful father to Kate, an only child.

Until lately. The last few years had been different, and then Mom leaving while Kate was finishing veterinary school. And suddenly she was really hearing her father's voice; not as a child would, but as an adult. He sounded . . . how? Regretful?

In the background she could hear a lot of noise; high-speed printers, perhaps. Chimes warning of something, and the constant ring of telephones and people talking; a lot of telephones, a lot of people.

Kate resigned herself. "You're blowing me off again, aren't you, Dad?"

"I'm so sorry, hon. You know how much I wanted to see you this weekend."

She believed that part of it, as far as it went. But he hadn't finished the sentence, so she did it for him. "I know, Dad, but it's a matter of national security. Right?"

"Sweetheart, please. We're swamped here, that's all. But it'll ease up, I can promise you that much."

"When?"

"Soon. Honest." Her dad let the word hang, and Kate really did understand. It was the damned CRS project he'd been assigned to. It was eating him alive. His wife had been the first casualty and Kate was beginning to wonder if she was next. She softened.

"I know, you can't talk about it." She glanced at Scott who had picked up a sterling picture frame and was trying the scanner on its bar code. But he was watching her, listening. "It's just that Scott was really looking forward to this."

The expression of relief on Scott's face was almost comical. He didn't want to admit it but he was having some trepidation about meeting Kate's father—*the* general, as he called him.

"Aw, Katie, I'm so sorry. I can't believe I still haven't met him."

"It's okay, Dad," Kate said. "You're bound to run into him at the wedding."

"Please, I'm still in a state of denial about that," General Brewster told his daughter. She could hear the wry note in his voice. He'd told her a couple of years ago that he was having trouble thinking of his little girl out there in the real world on her own. To him she was still the tomboy with pigtails and scabby knees who brought every stray or hurt animal that could fly, hop, slither, or swim home with her.

He definitely was having a much harder time accepting the fact that his only child was about to get married. Which was, Kate had to admit, just about how she was feeling right now.

"You're not the only one—" she said.

"Just a second, sweetheart," the general said, and Kate could hear that someone had come into her dad's office.

"Sorry to bother you, sir, but the Agency needs a fast turnaround on the last DoD promotionals."

"Right, the dog and pony show," General Brewster said. He was apparently holding a hand over the phone, but Kate could still hear the conversation. "When are they screening?"

"Tomorrow. One P.M.," the man said. Kate figured he was an aide. She thought she heard a door close.

"Dad? Are you still there? Dad?"

"I'm here, Katie," General Brewster said. He lowered his voice. "Are you okay, sweetheart? What's the matter?"

Scott had walked over to one of the clerks and was saying something to him.

"Nothing," Kate said, unsure even now just how much of this she wanted to tell her father. But she had no one else. "It's just that I don't know—"

The general said something to someone at his end, but then he was back. "Look, why don't you come see me out here this weekend? If Moses can't come to the mountain, maybe the mountain can come to him."

"I wish I could, but we have to meet with the minister, the wedding planner, and—"

"It's only a few hours away. Why don't you come to see me . . . you and Scott."

She looked up again. Scott had gotten into some kind of an argument with the clerk.

"Okay," she said, and she could hear the little girl tone creep into her voice. She wanted to be taken care of. She wanted someone else to take the responsibility for a change. For just a little while.

"Hey, kiddo, you know that you don't need me to pass judgment on this guy. You've done the right thing your whole life."

"I know," Kate said glumly. "Maybe that's the problem."

"You won't make a mistake," her father told her confidently. "You never do. I'm the luckiest father in the world, you know. I've never had to be afraid for my daughter."

Kate had to smile. She was on the verge of tears. Her father was still her Rock of Gibraltar.

"Listen, I hate to do this, but I gotta run. Come see me tomorrow. Promise?"

"We will," Kate said. "Bye, Dad. Love you."

"Love you too."

Cyber Research Systems
Edwards Air Force Base

General Brewster slowly hung up the telephone and thought about his daughter for a moment. He had told her a white lie. He *was* worried about her. This Scott person, whoever he was, really didn't matter. The trouble was with Kate herself. She had been distant just lately. Preoccupied, as if something was bothering her. Something that was apparently even more important than her upcoming marriage.

CRS operations was very busy this evening as it had been all day. Troubles seemed to be popping up just about everywhere throughout the civilian as well as military-use computer systems.

They'd expected some start-up troubles as they experimented with the Skynet system. But they had not expected this level of problems. And the system wasn't even fully booted up yet.

General Brewster knew that it was going to be another very long night.

He looked up and waved the project's chief engineer, Tony Flickinger, in. "Okay, what have we got?"

Flickinger, who'd graduated cum laude from MIT in the early nineties, made his mark with Microsoft, then came over to Cyberdyne to work with Miles Dyson. With Dyson's death and the dissolution of the old company, Flickinger transferred to the Cyber Research Systems operation, becoming the Skynet chief engineer four years ago. He was very good at his job. In fact, General Brewster reflected, Flickinger was practically Skynet himself. He knew more about the system and its potential than any man alive.

"It's not getting better," Flickinger said. He went to Brewster's computer terminal and brought up Skynet.

"This new computer virus is a tricky bastard. It's infected half the civilian Internet, as well as a lot of secondary military apps—payroll, inventory."

"Primary defense nets are still clean?"

Flickinger looked up. His thinning short-cropped hair had gone prematurely gray. With his round face and pale complexion he looked the part of a computer engineer who had spent most of his adult life in artificial light.

"So far the firewalls are holding up, but the Pentagon's proposed that we use our AI to scan the entire infrastructure, search and destroy any hint of the virus."

"I know, Tony. But it's like going after a fly with a bazooka."

Flickinger shrugged. To him this was just another engineering problem that needed solving. "Once the connection is made, it should only be a matter of minutes before Skynet is in charge of our national security."

"During which we'd put everything from satellites to missile silos under the control of a single computer system."

"The most intelligent system ever conceived."

Brewster shook his head. "I still prefer to keep humans in the loop. It's a huge step from weapons design to command and control. I'm not sure Skynet is ready."

The Skynet page came up on the monitor. It showed a graphic map of the western U.S. with strategic military installations connected by green lines. The display showed real-time connections of data interchange between systems. The lines pulsated with energy.

Each installation glowed comfortably green. ALL OP-

ERATIONS WITHIN PARAMETERS. OPERATIONS NORMAL.

But General Brewster was worried. At War College they'd studied worst-case scenarios in which U.S. strategic defense initiatives became short-circuited so that the nation's Nuclear Release Authority was bypassed.

Missiles flew.

The war began.

Los Angeles

"One day, it's all I'm asking, Scott," Kate tried to convince her fiancé. "It's no big deal. A couple hours out, a couple hours back. We'll be home in time to go out to dinner or something."

"I'm sorry, the computers are down," a clerk apologized, coming up to where they stood. She was an older woman in a stern business suit, glasses perched on her narrow nose, a gold chain from the stems around her neck. "And we're closing soon. Just write out your choices, and I'll input them into the registry in the morning."

"Okay, thanks," Scott said, taking the clipboard from her. She gave both of them a smile, then left.

Scott turned on Kate. He was mildly irritated, which for Scott was something. "I can't believe you told *the* general we'd drive all the way out to Mojave. Is this so he can show me how important he is?"

Kate touched his arm, a conciliatory gesture. "It won't be so bad."

Scott looked away to make sure no one was observing

what he would afterward call one of their little "tiffs." "It's just, I wanted to meet him on my own turf, you know?"

Kate turned away, irritated too. She didn't want to fight with Scott over her father. Not tonight. Maybe not ever. She picked up a brass picture frame with a photo of a romantic couple strolling hand-in-hand along a deserted beach in the moonlight.

"Yeah, sure," she muttered in answer to Scott's question. She didn't want to fight with him tonight. So, what did that say about their future?

She didn't know. She didn't know anything. And that was a terribly bleak prospect for her just now.

July 2029
Navajo Mountain

Lieutenant Colonel Jeff Parsons was dead. His body had lain beside his computer console in the second tier of consoles in the control room of the North American Aerospace Defense Command deep within the mountain for the past twenty-six years.

On Judgment Day those personnel caught inside were massacred when Skynet pumped all the oxygen out of the Redoubt, replacing it with pure nitrogen from the spare liquid nitrogen stores used to super-cool the high-power low-mass equipment.

Parsons's body lay on its side, its face dark purple, its flesh surprisingly intact after more than a quarter of a century. But rotting meat required oxygen, of which there was none inside the mountain.

Skynet was indifferent to gas or gas volumes, as it was indifferent to lighting, so the control rooms and various other spaces within the complex were lit only by the indicators and screens on electronic consoles and panels.

But the AI was sensitive to heat and humidity, so Navajo Mountain Redoubt was kept at a comfortable twenty degrees Celsius at twenty percent relative humidity.

Parsons's eyes were open, but neither he nor the dozens of other corpses with him were aware that the cathedral hush of the large domed room was broken when impossibly fast streams of data crossed the main status board and a pair of Advanced Utility T-20 server robots trundled off an elevator.

Between them, walking flat-footed, back arched, head held high as if she were a soldier being escorted by the Praetorian Guard, was what Parsons would have considered the most perfect nude woman he'd ever seen.

But Parsons was dead, and Skynet was indifferent to considerations of human beauty except where such considerations were germane to the parameters of a mission.

She was a T-X, Enhanced Logic Weapons Systems Cybernetic Warrior/Infiltration Unit. T-X, for short.

An absolutely brilliant creation of superior intelligence, beauty, speed, adaptability, lethality, survivability, and supreme indifference, T-X was Skynet's latest advance in projection-of-power technology.

Stripped to her utilitarian battle chassis, protected by malleable ceramic/titanium armor, she was practically unstoppable on the battlefield, as the human resistance fighters under the commands of Colonel Steve Earle and Lieutenant Joel Benson had already found out.

Adorned with her infiltration trappings: muscles, sinews, blood vessels, skin, hair, T-X would be just as deadly among the pre-Judgment Day human population as she was on the current battlefields.

Possibly even deadlier if she could reach and eliminate the right targets.

Although she weighed in excess of 150 kilos, her footfalls were whisper soft across the bare tile floor as she threaded her way through the corpses and computer consoles to a transmission sphere the twin of the one at the old CRS facility twelve hundred kilometers to the west.

The T-20 robots that had escorted her backed off. T-X assumed the position, one knee and two hands on the pad as the sphere closed.

Her head bowed, eyes staring straight down, she waited with complete indifference. One minute, one hundred years, it did not matter.

Skynet's AI powered up the Continuum Transporter's circuits without fanfare, and seconds later the chamber took on a luminescent, electric blue aura.

T-X disappeared.

July 2003
Los Angeles

All the stores along Rodeo Drive were closed, only a few eating establishments and night spots in the vicinity were still doing business.

Traffic was light, the occasional car or SUV, one of them with a Bose stereo system cranked to full volume and bass, where during the day the street teemed with cars and with shoppers all looking for the ultimate dress, the perfect shoes, the neatest toy.

An older woman in tight crop pants, with an artistically clipped full poodle on a leash, walked past the window displays of Sharron Batten: Fine Resort Wear, Beverly Hills, Palm Beach, Cannes.

The woman glanced at the mannequins modeling clothes that only a size four would wear, and then only on the French Riviera. A large black-and-white poster hung from the ceiling and was cleverly backlit so it seemed as if the model standing hipshot, a thumb hooked in the elastic band of her brief bikini bottom, was illuminated by the setting sun. The caption read I LIKE THIS LOOK!

The gauze print beach shirt on one of the mannequins ruffled in a sudden small breeze. The scarf around the neck of another moved.

A mist began to fill the window display, until a bright blue sphere suddenly materialized in a burst of lightning and intense heat that instantly melted the plastic mannequins, burned through a sizable area of concrete floor, and melted a hole three meters in diameter in the plate-glass window.

T-X raised her head to catalog her new surroundings, numbers and graphs crossing her head-up display with a rapidity that no human could follow. She rose gracefully from her kneeling position, and heedless of the still-glowing concrete and molten glass dripping from the window, she stepped out onto the sidewalk.

In the distance to the southwest, down Rodeo Drive, T-X's infrared systems picked up the heat signatures of a woman and a much smaller quadrupedal mammal classified as *Canis familiaris,* and immediately rejected either as possible infiltration personas.

She looked northeast. A ground conveyance, classified as a Lexus SC430, was parked in front of a concrete, steel, and glass building, with the legend BARCLAYS in brass. The heat signatures from the automobile's engine compartment and exhaust system were consistent with a condition known as idling.

A secondary heat source stood approximately eight meters to the north of the automobile. It was a female human. T-X enhanced her optical system and overlaid the mission's requirements. The female, who was attempting to effect a transaction between herself and an incredibly primitive computer via a small plastic card in which were programmed several hundred bytes of rudimentary information, was not a currently listed target, but she was of the proper weight, height, physical shape, and apparent age for mission purposes.

The ATM machine beeped several times, and a crude, machine-generated voice said, "Sorry, we are unable to process transactions at this time," as T-X crossed the street.

Nancy Nebel was only mildly irritated. She'd never had much luck with machines, partly because she wasn't interested and partly because that's what men were supposed to do for a girl. At thirty-two she was what her friends in the business called a looker. Blond, blue-eyed, with a knockout figure, she was dressed this evening in a rust-colored leather jacket and skintight pants, beneath which she wore a black lace thong and lace Wonderbra. Why give 'em brains when all they wanted was cleavage, was her motto.

And it had worked so far.

Nancy put the gold American Express card back in her purse, and got behind the wheel of her car, the reasons she needed the money tonight already forgotten. She had just enough time to get over to Spago before Lenny got too worried about her.

She looked up as she was about to reach for the gearshift lever in time to see a tall, very sexy blond woman, stark naked, walking up the sidewalk as if she didn't have a care in the world.

A little thrill of fear tickled Nancy's stomach. Something was way off base here. She leaned out of the car. "Hey! Are you okay?"

The woman didn't miss a beat.

Nancy fumbled for the cell phone on the dash. "Did somebody attack you?" she asked the woman. "I'll call nine-one-one—"

T-X stopped at the driver's side door and Nancy looked up at her makeup-free, totally flawless complexion. The woman's breasts were firm and perfectly formed. Her stomach was completely flat. She was perfect. Too perfect.

"I like this car," T-X said.

It started to dawn on Nancy that the broad was some kind of bad news. Somebody's bimbo on a bad trip. "You're on something, aren't you?"

T-X reached in and gently caressed the lapel of Nancy's leather jacket. "I like this look."

"What—" Nancy said, rearing back. This was big trouble. She wanted to get away, right now.

T-X placed a thumb and forefinger on either side of the woman's spinal column at the base of her skull, and pinched. The bone crushed easily.

T-X was not programmed to be squeamish. She dressed in the woman's clothes, including the lace underwear.

When she was done, she got in the driver's seat and studied the dash instruments, the steering wheel, shift mechanism, and pedals for a moment, her processors building a more complete picture of the engineering of the machine than even the original Lexus engineers had.

She dropped it into drive and sped off, peeling rubber as she accelerated, a map of the Los Angeles freeway system appearing in her head-up display.

The telephone rang. T-X answered it, perfectly imitating Nancy Nebel's voice. "Hello?"

A man came on. "Honey, I'm at the restaurant, where are—"

T-X broke the connection. An extremely rapid string of numbers crossed her display, which she entered on the cell phone's keypad, her fingers moving faster than any human's could move.

A crash of static came over the speaker as the connection was made. T-X opened her mouth and emitted a series of eleven beep tones. The distant circuit rang once, followed by the squeal of a high-speed modem. T-X made the audible connection with the proper signal, and moments later data began to stream back and forth between T-X and a Los Angeles County database computer downtown.

Tiny lines of text along with dozens of charts passed T-X's head-up display: names, addresses, medical, financial, and employment data along with images, mostly head shots.

The photographs of two humans, one male, one female, youngish-looking, lingered for a full second in T-X's display, followed by an address in the foothills above Westwood.

T-X was in no apparent hurry, but she drove very fast, and for normal human response times and abilities, apparently recklessly, weaving in and out of traffic, even running red lights when her sensors registered and computed no obstructions.

She jumped onto the Hollywood Freeway, but got off almost immediately because of the traffic. Her onboard navigational systems booted up, automatically merging with the Skynet system currently in orbit for this era.

She was working her way through streets of strip malls and businesses, traffic sometimes heavy, but most of the time light.

An automobile with lights mounted on a roof rack shot out from a used car lot and fell in behind T-X.

She glanced in the rearview mirror with one eye, her

sensors scanning and evaluating the new phenomenon. The automobile was a Los Angeles Police squad car. Its red and white lights were flashing; its siren whooped several times.

She was being pursued.

"You, in the silver Lexus! Slow down and pull over!" the amplified voice of the lone police officer boomed from the radio unit. "Pull over immediately!"

T-X considered the situation for something less than one millisecond before getting off the accelerator and braking to a hard stop as she pulled over to the side of the street across from what looked like an office or business complex of some sort behind a tall iron fence. Brightly colored graffiti was painted over all the brick walls inside the empty parking area.

At the end of the block a large, well lit billboard for Victoria's Secret displayed a beautiful model wearing nothing more than a wide, toothy smile, a very low-cut bra, and brief panties.

T-X was aware of the squad car stopping behind her, and of the lone male officer getting out of the car and approaching. He was beefy with a square face and short-cropped hair.

She was also aware of the Victoria's Secret advertisement and what its significance was vis-à-vis the human male-female sexual relationship.

She flexed her shoulder and back muscles so that her breasts became more prominent, turned her head, looked up, and smiled just as the cop reached her.

"Good evening, Officer," she said.

His eyes strayed to her breasts. "Um, lady? You know how fast you were going?"

"Eighty-two point three miles per hour," T-X said.

The cop had to smile. This was one for the books, something he could tell at the precinct house. Christ, but she was built. "It's a thirty-mile-an-hour zone," he said. He'd opened his ticket book, but flipped it shut. How could you ticket perfection? "I really oughta write you a ticket here."

T-X glanced at the cop's shiny patent leather utility belt. She catalogued the sidearm as a Sig-Sauer P226, with a fifteen-round detachable box magazine. Total length was 196 mm, its weight empty was 750 g, the cartridge was a 9mm Parabellum with a muzzle velocity of 335 meters per second with the 115-grain JHP round.

She smiled again at the cop whose name tag read BARNES. "I like that gun."

The Valley

He had trashed his bike, permanently this time. The frame was bent all to hell, the gas tank punctured, the engine case cracked when it hit the boulder, both wheels folded like pretzels.

Riding in the rear of the ratty flatbed truck back down into the valley, John Connor had plenty of time to feel sorry for himself, and to be pissed off as well by his own stupidity.

He knew what his mother would have said about it; she had been the one talking all the time about how fate was what we made of it. Not the other way around. He had done it to himself, this time, with no help from anyone.

Any of her biker boyfriends would have laughed, clapped him on the shoulder, passed him the tequila, and said something like: "Next time you go rodding around in the middle of the night, maybe you should wear a parachute." Or something like: "Did that big, bad deer knock you on your ass, kid?"

There'd be no sympathy from anyone, but there

would be a grudging acceptance that he'd had the cojones to pull off such a stunt in the first place and the bald-ass luck to survive it.

The stuff from his packs had been scattered halfway down the hill to the ocean, and it had taken him the better part of two hours, climbing up and down in the loose sand and rocks, fighting his pains, to find most of it and get back up to the Drive.

It'd only taken one minute, however, from the moment he'd reached the tangled mess that had been his bike, until he came to the conclusion that it was beyond repair. He might have been able to salvage some parts, but he'd been unable to find his tools or flashlight, and he didn't have the heart to lug around a bunch of useless crap.

He'd had the balls, or the stupidity, to pull the stunt, but he had to wonder if he'd been lucky after all. If there was no purpose in living, then why live at all?

It had been a recurrent theme of his. Maybe it was time for him to finally do something about it.

Put up or shut up, his foster mom had told him once. That was when his real mother was in the nuthouse up at Pescadero.

The first vehicle that had come along had been the flatbed loaded with ten Mexican laborers nearly blind drunk, laughing and singing.

They had come from one party and were headed to a sister's house somewhere over near Van Nuys. None of them noticed that John was banged up, his hands raw with road rash, jeans torn up, blood oozing from a long gash in his leg.

Never mind that the beer was piss warm, and the tequila was so cheap that kerosene would have tasted better. They were willing to share.

They had no trouble deciding who and what they were, or where their lives were going. They had never been fed any delusions about becoming a world leader. Nor probably had they ever been the target of some machine, sent on an assassination mission.

They had come down out of the hills and passed under I-101 before Connor looked up out of his morose thoughts and became aware of where he was.

The neighborhood was blue collar, industrial. They passed a small bank and a supermarket, and at the end of the block, across from what looked like a construction site or maybe a place where they stored heavy construction equipment, was an animal hospital.

John flexed his leg, which had stiffened up on the long ride, and fresh blood oozed out of the wound. He needed help, but he wasn't willing to go to the emergency room of some hospital. There would be too many questions. And that was the one thing he was very bad at, answering questions, especially the kind that cops were bound to ask. He had no permanent address, no real money, not even a proper ID. He was in no one's database, so far as he knew. He had never applied for a loan or a credit card. He had never owned a house. In fact he'd never owned anything, except for his bike, which he bought from a down-and-out biker who needed the cash for drugs. If the cops started digging into who and what he was, he figured that he would be in trouble.

He pulled himself up and pounded a fist on the roof of the cab. The driver stuck his head out the window and looked over his shoulder at John.

"*¿Qué?*"

"*Acá me bajo,*" John shouted at him.

"*Sí, sí,*" the driver said, and he pulled over, bumping up on the curb and then down again. Everyone laughed. This was great fun.

The sign on the building read UNIVERSAL RENTALS, and behind the chain-link fence a big yellow mobile crane, its massive telescoping boom fixed over the truck's cab like a tank's cannon, loomed over the neighborhood.

Across the street a small glass-fronted building was lit only from the outside. The sign on the front read EMERY ANIMAL HOSPITAL.

Connor gathered his tattered packs and bedroll and climbed painfully down from the back of the truck.

"*Gracias,*" he called to the driver, who waved back.

"*Sí, sí,*" the man said, and the others waved as the truck took off in a cloud of smoke and dust, leaving Connor standing alone in the middle of the street.

There was no traffic here at this hour, and after the truck was gone the night turned silent.

Connor limped across the street and looked through the front windows into the darkened reception room of the animal clinic. It was unlikely that a place this small would have a night watchman, but you could never tell.

He made his way around to a back loading area. A small window looked into a kennel where animals undergoing treatment were kept overnight.

He pulled a towel from one of his packs, wrapped it around a fist, and smashed the window.

Immediately the bigger dogs started barking and growling wildly, while the small animals yipped and a few of the sicker ones mewled or whined.

"Shh, it's okay, guys," Connor told them. He reached inside, undid the latch, and lifted the window. "It's okay," he called. He dropped his packs inside, then climbed in after them.

The kennel was filled with animal smells only partially masked by the odor of a strong disinfectant. Water was running somewhere, and the compressor motor for what was probably a refrigerator kicked on. But there were no alarms, and the dogs were already calming down, more curious now than frightened or aggressive.

There was a row of cages, some large, some small, a lot of them empty. The animals here were sick, some of them banged up as badly as Connor. He felt an instant empathy with them.

A big chocolate Lab, its left rear leg in a cast, looked up with mournful eyes. John offered the dog the back of his hand, then scratched it behind the ears. The animal almost groaned out loud in ecstasy.

Love at first sight, Connor thought, following the line of cages through a door into what appeared to be the clinic's medical storage area. The room was small and cluttered with cardboard boxes, many of them unopened, file cabinets, large cases, and glass-fronted supply cabinets.

"Bingo," he said under his breath. It was exactly what he was looking for.

He went back for his packs, then jimmied open the glass doors of one of the supply cabinets that held tranquilizers, gauze, antibiotic creams, syringes, boxes of sutures, splints, catheters, and an entire shelf of prescription drugs.

He picked one marked TORBUTROL. FOR RELIEF OF PAIN. VETERINARY USE ONLY. He shook out a handful of the pills and dry swallowed them. If they didn't work on humans, he figured he would find out about it soon enough when he dropped down on all fours and started howling at the moon,

From the time he, and the T-800 sent back to protect him, busted his mom out of the sanitarium, Connor had essentially been on his own. He'd been thirteen then, and before his fourteenth birthday he could disassemble, clean, repair, reassemble, and fire more than two dozen different types of weapons, explosives, and even Light Antitank Weapons and Stinger ground-to-air handheld missiles.

It had been quite the education. He could calculate blast radius damage for various plastique explosives, but he had never heard of the Magna Carta let alone the year it was signed.

And he was still alone, he thought, grabbing sutures, gauze, alcohol, disinfectant ointment, and bandages.

He dropped his pants, cleaned the six-inch gash in his thigh with alcohol, then opened one of the suture packs and began sewing up the wound, the animal narcotic already fuzzing out the worst of the pain.

Mojave Desert

Terminator moved across the open desert like a ship on the sea, homing in on a distant port that his onboard sensors had detected hours ago.

He felt neither heat nor cold nor impatience with the duration of this primary phase of the mission. He had been sent back to execute an operation. Nothing would stop him. No power on earth could divert him from his path, except for the destruction of his neural circuitry or the complete destruction of his battle chassis.

If and when he needed information on file for comparison, measurements, identifications, or decisions, his CPU was alerted to fire a series of networks that would act like an electronic adrenaline to his system.

Without breaking his long, distance-eating stride, Terminator's infrared, optical, electromagnetic emissions, and directed audio sensors continued to pick up a melange of data: heat signatures from dozens of ground conveyances—cars, trucks, and motorcycles—electronic noise from what he computed as excited neon gas, sixty Hz common electrical circuitry, some high-frequency broadcasts to and from portable communications devices called cell phones, dozens of human body heat sources mixed in ever-changing blocking and additive patterns, and combinations of sounds of mixed frequencies at varying rhythmic speeds that he understood to be music.

He enhanced his optical system, focusing on a neon sign, DESERT STAR, in front of a ramshackle building.

A highway ran directly past the building, which Terminator classified as a roadhouse/drinking establishment, common to many parts of the continental U.S.; most specifically this variety was to be found in the West and desert Southwest. A gathering place for human ritualized mating and aggressive behavior, catering mostly to a narrow socio-economic range of people.

His CPU pulled up a variety of programmed response patterns and overlaid them on his basic real-time mode. His head came up, he rose slightly on the balls of his feet, and a small, sardonic smile played at the edges of his mouth.

The T-800 series, which had been modeled after a U.S. Marine Corps chief master sergeant, was, in its infiltration mode, a handsome cyborg, with short dark hair, broad craggy features, prominent nose, and deep set intense eyes. It was built with the musculature of a world-class athlete, perhaps an Iron Man gold medalist, with strong pecs, a washboard stomach, narrow waist, and massive but well sculpted thighs and biceps. The Marine sergeant who had been a man's man, who epitomized speed, agility, expertise, reliability, and dedication had been perfectly translated into the various model T-800s.

He did not hesitate at the side of the highway, but stepped up on the pavement that was finally cool after the day's desert heat, and strode directly across the filled parking lot to the front entrance of the rustic redwood bar and club.

The music was very loud, thumping with a heavy bass. By the sounds of the cheering and laughing coming from inside, the bar was packed and people were having a good time.

A large, beefy man in jeans, leather vest, and broad-brimmed cowboy hat sat on a stool next to the main entrance. His eyes narrowed slightly when he spotted the nude Terminator, but he showed no real surprise.

He languidly got to his feet as Terminator approached. He stepped directly in front of the door. He was six five at three hundred pounds, and he looked mean.

He motioned to the left. "You're supposed to go round back."

Terminator gave no indication that he had heard the bouncer, simply sweeping the man aside with one hand as if he were batting away an irritating insect.

"What the hell—"

Terminator pushed open the saloon doors and stepped inside to a loud, smoky room filled with at least two hundred women all cheering, whistling, applauding, and stomping on the wooden floorboards for the male stripper who was just prancing off the small stage at the back. Music blared from big speakers suspended from the ceiling and bracketing the stage. Glittering curtains were lit by red and green and blue and pink rotating baby

spots. A large sign attached to the back curtains read
LADIES NIGHT.

Terminator scanned the audience. A few of the
women had turned around and spotted him. Overlaid on
his head-up display were the size and shape parameters
for clothing to fit his frame. Most of the sizes and none
of the styles that the women were wearing would do,
though many of them were dressed androgynously in
jeans, denim shirts, and boots.

He also correctly catalogued that his earlier assess-
ment about the probable socio-economic class of the people who might frequent such a club as this was correct.
In many instances humans were too predictable.

A buxom, floozy blonde, wearing thick makeup and
long, fake eyelashes, got unsteadily to her feet and clapped
her hands over her head, a toothy grin from ear to ear.
"Shake it, baby!" she shouted.

Terminator's sensors evaluated her size. Her short
denim skirt, boots, and fringed blouse might fit him, but
his head-up display read INAPPROPRIATE.

A much smaller, younger redhead, nearer at hand,
looked Terminator's body up and down, her eyes lingering
on his anatomically correct groin area, a lascivious grin
on her narrow face. She was mostly inebriated. "Need a
date?" she asked.

Other women had spotted him now, and they were
jumping to their feet, applauding and giving catcalls and
whistles. If this was a part of the show, it was the best
part, most of them were thinking.

A loud, super-rhythmic song suddenly blared from

the speakers. Terminator correctly identified it as a piece called "Macho Man," performed by the Village People.

A tall, huskily built male stripper bounced out onto the stage. He was dressed in a cap, a red scarf around his neck, and biker boots and leathers.

Terminator turned to look at the man. His head-up display instantly evaluated a match. He strode through the crowd of cheering women to the stage.

"Take your clothes off," he told the stripper, who shot him an interested smile, but shook his head.

"Patience, honey."

Terminator climbed onto the stage, and the women, still believing that this was part of the show, went wild; cheering louder than before, whistling their encouragement.

"Whoa, bitch, wait your turn!" the stripper said. He was already into his act, swaying his hips and shoulders. Terminator was nice, but just now he was nothing but competition. Irritating.

"Your clothes," Terminator repeated adamantly.

The stripper stuck a hand directly in Terminator's face. "Talk to the hand," he suggested, and he turned away.

Terminator grabbed the stripper's hand, the wrist crunching like a Shredded Wheat biscuit. "Now."

The stripper screamed in pain and fear, stumbling back a step as Terminator let go. This was far worse than competition. The son of a bitch didn't have an ounce of decency. He was probably on something. The stripper hurriedly pulled off his cap and kerchief, then the jacket, awkwardly because his wrist was dislocated or maybe broken. But his blood was pumping with raw terror so he wasn't feeling much.

The women were on their feet, crazier than ever. This was by far the very best show that any of them had ever seen. It looked so real!

Terminator donned the stripper's clothing, the boots a little tight, then turned without another word, strode across the stage and through the curtain to a back storage area that had been converted into a dressing room for the acts.

A few of the strippers did a double take, realizing that the man in Larry's outfit was definitely not Larry. He didn't have *the* walk.

"Macho Man" was still playing, and the women were still screaming, as Terminator stepped out the back door into the parking lot.

The heavyset blonde from the audience came right behind him. "Hey, you!" she shouted drunkenly.

Terminator turned to regard her, but he said nothing.

"Will you be back?" the woman demanded.

He looked at her for a long moment, then turned and scanned the parking lot, almost immediately spotting a big-wheeled Dodge pickup truck, an NRA sticker on the rear bumper, a shotgun in a rear window rack.

He headed directly for it, but caught his reflection in the window of a car. He stopped and looked at his image, bringing up one of the memories that John Connor had supplied of what T-800 had looked like twelve years ago. He took off the stripper's star-shaped sunglasses and tossed them aside. He did the same with the cap and red bandanna. His current image now nearly matched the previous overlay.

He walked to the truck and without hesitation poked his fist through the driver's side window, opened the door, and climbed into the cab. The truck's alarm system shrieked and the lights flashed. Ignoring them, Terminator casually ripped the ignition switch from the steering column, which silenced the alarm, and hot-wired the start and run systems.

The truck's engine roared to life. Terminator's eyes lit on a pair of sunglasses on the dash. He put them on, dropped the truck into gear, and hammered the gas pedal.

The truck shot out of the parking lot, spewing a rooster tail of gravel behind it.

As Terminator bumped up onto the highway and headed west, toward Los Angeles, he looked in the rearview mirror in time to see the bouncer in the broad-brimmed cowboy hat running after him, a fist raised in the air.

Westwood

Luring the police officer Barnes away from his duties and killing him had been ridiculously easy, though T-X could not think of the act in such terms. It was simply a minor extension of her main mission plan.

She had unbuttoned her shirt and lifted her bra. "Do you like these?"

The cop's eyes had widened, and he nodded stupidly. "Yeah, nice. What do you have in mind?"

She smiled. "Follow me," she said, and the cop had followed her into a dark corner of a hardware store parking lot.

T-X glanced at the Sig-Sauer lying on the passenger seat. It was a well-crafted, efficient weapon for this era. There was only the one magazine of ammunition, which gave her fifteen rounds. But it would be more than sufficient for her mission.

The machine-generated voice of the GPS navigational unit in the Lexus advised, "Left turn ahead."

T-X glanced at the in-dash screen on which a map of the upscale Westwood area of Los Angeles was displayed.

She had entered one of the addresses from her program. This first one was for a number on a side street in the foothills above Santa Monica Boulevard, four blocks away, according to the nav system.

Except for the good sex, Bill Anderson decided that he was starting to get real tired of Tammy Triggs, his current love interest. But then at seventeen who had to be choosy? St. Ed's was loaded with hot girls, and even his twelve-year-old sister, Liz, once admitted that her brother was a chick magnet.

He got up from the couch in the den where he and Tammy had gone to be alone and watch TV. "Want another beer?" He was tall, with a lean build that stood him well on the basketball court. With his blond hair and blue eyes he was one hundred percent California.

"Sure," Tammy said distractedly. She had found Liz's stupid robot dog, Aibo, and had been playing with it for the past hour. Instead of making out.

Bill went into the palatial, burnished aluminum and Mexican tile kitchen, grabbed a couple of Buds from the fridge, and headed back to the den.

Dad was in New York on business. Mom was at a Botox party somewhere in Beverly Hills, and Liz was upstairs in her room doing homework.

Which should have left him Tammy, whose parents were both out of town.

He stopped in the Italianate marble hall that ran the

width of the upscale twenty-two-room house on an acre and a half of prime real estate and glanced at Tammy's reflection in the big mirror across from the den. She was down on all fours, coaxing the plastic dog with the remote control unit.

The television was acting up again. Lines of ones and zeroes crossed the wavering images. A newscaster was saying something about a super virus.

". . . widespread outages in the global digital network have prompted rumors of a new computer super virus."

Bill figured it was probably some loser in Covina or down in La Puente, bored out of his skull with no prospects, hacking the system.

He brought the beers into the den and set them on the coffee table as CNN continued the late breaking story.

"Wall Street analysts are confident, however, that high tech issues will—"

Bill switched channels to the war of the Battlebots. Then flipped again, and again. He had to admit that he was bored out of his skull too.

The number on the steel security gate matched the head-up display T-X was reading. She pulled to a stop at the security keypad and reached to it with the index finger of her left hand.

Nothing happened for a brief moment, but then the liquid metal skin retracted from the finger, and a 1.6 mm titanium alloy drill bit emerged from the fingertip and cut into the keypad's cover plate like a hot knife through soft butter, but with a high-pitched, almost inaudible whine. A narrow blue aura of the same angstrom length as emitted by the Continuum Transporter flowed through the tiny drill bit into the gate and security system.

T-X transferred a stream of data into the system, then withdrew her hand and the gate opened.

"Tammy, shut the stupid dog off, would you?" Bill asked.

She looked up as headlights flashed across the windows from the driveway below.

Bill jumped off the couch, his heart in his throat. "Shit, my mom's home. Hide the beer!"

He switched off the television as Tammy grabbed the half-dozen beer cans from the coffee table and started stashing them under the long sectional.

Out in the hall he checked the mirror to make sure he didn't look too guilty, at the same moment he heard high heels coming up the sidewalk. About twice a week his mom either forgot the garage door opener or forgot how to use it or was too drunk to care, so she left the Mercedes in the front and rang the doorbell.

This was one of those times.

Bill touched the alarm keypad but the system was already off, and the front door opened without the lock release delay.

A slender blond woman, in a sharp-looking leather suit and high-heeled boots, stood in the glow of the front light, a killer smile on her narrow face. She wasn't half bad for an older woman. A Lexus convertible was parked in the driveway.

"Um . . . you must be looking for my mom. She's out—"

"Elizabeth and William Anderson?" T-X asked politely.

Bill glanced over his shoulder. Tammy had come to the hall. He turned back. "I'm Bill, my sister's upstairs. Are you from the school, or something—?" He was confused. This wasn't making sense.

The smile left T-X's face at the same moment she slammed the heel of her hand into Bill's solar plexus, shoving him violently off his feet back into the hall.

Tammy stepped back, her hand to her mouth, not completely sure of what she was witnessing. But it was bad.

T-X pulled the Sig-Sauer from her pocket and fired three shots into Bill's chest as he started to rise, killing him instantly.

Tammy screamed, turned on her heel, and raced for the back of the house.

T-X let her go. The young woman was not in the mission program.

She stepped over Bill's corpse, and turned left up the stairs to the upper floor. Music came from a room at the end of the corridor. T-X followed the sounds to their source, opening the door into a girl's bedroom.

Elizabeth Anderson, Liz to her friends, looked up from the video game she was beating on her television.

She was a cute girl, round face, innocent eyes. She cocked her head quizzically. "Who are you?"

T-X raised the Sig-Sauer and put one round precisely into the lower left center of the girl's chest, the heavy 9mm bullet shattering the heart.

The Valley

The pager beeped at 5:06 A.M. as text crossed the tiny screen.

Kate opened her eyes. It was still dark. The pager lying on the nightstand on her side of the bed was beeping. Her eyes went to the luminous numbers on the alarm clock. It was practically the middle of the night. The best part. The last hour of sleep before she had to get up to go to work.

But it was Saturday. "Dammit," she muttered under her breath.

She grabbed the pager and squinted at the illuminated screen. The message: a.n.i.m.a.l ... e.m.e.r.g.e.n.c.y. scrolled across the display, repeating the same two words. The alarm system at the clinic was keyed to noise. If the animals got upset and started to make a racket it might mean that something was seriously wrong with one of them. And Kate was nothing if not a conscientious animal doctor.

She shut off the pager and got out of bed. Scott stirred and reached out a hand to her.

"What's going on?" he mumbled, still mostly asleep.

"I've got to go to the clinic," Kate said, pulling underwear out of the dresser. "It's an emergency."

She pulled off her nightshirt and hurriedly put on bra and panties, then got a shirt and slacks from the closet.

Scott got up on one elbow and looked at the clock. "It's five in the morning."

"I'll be back before you're up," Kate said, pulling on her slacks and tucking in her shirt. She stepped into her shoes and half stumbled, half hopped over to the bed. She leaned down and gave him a kiss.

Scott lay back, then turned over and was sound asleep by the time Kate grabbed a light jacket and headed out the door.

Early morning work traffic had already started to pick up as Kate drove the two miles over to the clinic, but it took her only a few minutes.

She'd gotten rid of her lime green VW bug six months ago when Scott moved in, so when she was on animal business she used the clinic's Toyota Tundra pickup with its tan cap and the Emery logo on the side. It was the only sensible solution because she sometimes made commercial calls, mostly to pet stores, and a few times to farms outside the valley.

It was satisfying work, most of the time. Animals were a lot more straightforward than people. They might be vicious sometimes, but they were always honest and up front. Especially the dogs. You always knew where you stood with them.

She parked in front and as soon as she got out of the truck she could hear the racket in the kennel, and her gut tightened. The last time this happened some junkie had broken into the place looking for drugs. The cops had shown up just ahead of Kate and had found the guy passed out in the reception area. Stoned on something. The dogs had gone wild.

She should have called the cops, but she had her cell phone and if need be 911 would dispatch a unit out here within minutes.

Kate let herself in through the front door, locking it behind her. She flipped on the lights and headed to the back. The dogs were barking like mad.

"Cool it, guys, it's just me," Kate said, heading down the hall to the supply room and kennel.

She pushed through the frosted glass doors, flipped on the lights, and tossed her keys and cell phone atop the file cabinet. Turning, she spotted the jimmied supply cabinet that had obviously been rummaged.

"Great. Junkies," she said, walking over to check out what was missing. An empty Torbutrol bottle was lying on the floor. She bent down to pick it up and spotted a splash of blood.

A trail of blood led across the room to the shadows in a corner. Surgical supplies were laid out on top of a box, bloody gauze on the floor, an empty suture set bag discarded.

Kate straightened up and stepped back, a little queasiness roiling in her stomach. Whoever it was had probably cut themselves breaking in.

She turned and reached for her cell phone as a man about her own age, but beat-up, like he'd been in some kind of an accident, limped out from behind a stack of dog food boxes.

"Please don't do that," Connor said, his voice a little slurred.

Kate's fear evaporated, changing into anger. "I suppose you're the asshole who ripped us off last week."

"No. That'd be some other asshole."

Kate edged nearer to the file cabinet and reached for her cell phone, but Connor pulled a pistol from his jacket and pointed it at her. His hand was unsteady and his eyes were bleary. Kate figured it was the Torbutrol.

"I can't let you call the cops," he said. "Sorry."

Kate stepped back from the file cabinet, and gave Connor a closer scrutiny. He looked as if he hadn't had a decent meal or a decent night's sleep in a long time. His eyes had a—she searched for a word. He looked haunted.

"It was an accident," he explained. "I just—needed medicine."

"There's an emergency clinic a half mile—"

"I can't do that," Connor cut her off.

Kate held up the empty Torbutrol bottle. "How much did you take?"

"Enough."

Kate shook her head. "Well, you took the wrong thing. This is the stuff we use to chemically neuter dogs."

Connor laughed. It was obvious he didn't believe her. But she kept her gaze steady, as if she thought he was stupid, and she felt sorry for him.

Suddenly he wasn't so sure. His eyes dropped to the pill bottle in her hand.

Kate tossed it at him. Instinctively he tried to catch it, momentarily losing his balance. She snatched the pistol from his hand, skipped back out of his reach, and pointed it at him.

"Take it easy," he said, raising a hand as if to ward off a blow.

"Back," she told him.

Connor stumbled backward through the double doors into the kennel where the dogs had finally started to quiet down. A few of them whined when they recognized Kate, but the animals were uncertain of what was going on.

Kate motioned toward one of the empty cages for large dogs. "I want you inside."

"No way—"

Kate raised the pistol. "Now."

Connor reluctantly did as he was ordered, his leg very painful. It was obvious he was watching for her to make a mistake. And it was just as obvious that he was in no shape to do anything about it, if she did. Not until the effects of the Torbutrol began to wear off.

Kate slammed the cage door shut, and dropped the latch. Now the cage was impossible to open from inside, and she allowed herself to relax for the first time.

She hunched down in front of the cage and looked at him. There was something familiar . . . something she couldn't quite put her finger on ... something bothersome.

"Look, this isn't what you think," Connor told her.

At that moment the buzzer at the front door went off. Someone had seen the lights in the reception room and had brought a sick animal.

"Yeah, right," she said.

She got up and went back into the storage room where she set the pistol aside and got her cell phone. Suddenly she had it! She knew! And it was like someone had dropped a brick on her head.

She turned on her heel and went back into the kennel. Connor looked up at her expectantly.

"Mike Kripke's basement," she said.

The front buzzer was going crazy, and the dogs were starting to get agitated again.

"What?" Connor asked, confused. "What does that mean?"

Kate shook her head in amazement, then went to find out what idiot was at the front door at this hour.

When she was gone, Connor tried for the latch, but it was just beyond his reach. He braced his back against the rear bars and kicked at the door with no results.

"Beautiful," he muttered.

North Hollywood

T-X waited until a garbage truck lumbered past, then turned into the takeout driveway of an all-night fast-food restaurant.

Twenty minutes ago she had telephoned the home number of Maria Barrera in Reseda, which she had downloaded from the L.A. County welfare database. Her Spanish was perfect, but Mrs. Barrera said that her son wasn't home. He was at work.

"He's a good boy. He's been no trouble. Please."

"Where is he working, Mrs. Barrera?" T-X asked politely.

"Jim's Burgers. It's in North Hollywood. Please, he's a good boy."

There were no cars in line as T-X pulled up to the menu board and speaker, and only a couple of Hispanic kids with their low-riders in the parking lot.

"Welcome to Jim's Burgers, can I take your order?" The voice was of a young, Hispanic male.

"José Barrera?" T-X asked.

"Um . . . yeah."

T-X pulled forward to the order window as Barrera leaned out to see what was going on. He looked to be in his late teens or early twenties. He wore a blue hat and blue shirt with the restaurant's logo.

T-X looked up at the boy and smiled. His name tag read Barrera. Her head-up display showed a match.

She had the Sig-Sauer on her lap. She lifted it and fired two shots into the young man's face, then laid the gun on the passenger seat, drove past the pickup window, around the restaurant, and back out onto the street where she accelerated smoothly into the night.

Her head-up display showed a grid:

```
ANDERSON, WILLIAM - TERMINATED
ANDERSON, ELIZABETH - TERMINATED
BARRERA, JOSÉ - TERMINATED
BREWSTER, KATHERINE - OPEN
CONNOR, JOHN - OPEN
```

The Katherine Brewster line was highlighted, and a file came up with photographs as well as home and work addresses and phone numbers.

She entered Katherine Brewster's home number into the cell phone. After five rings it was finally answered by a man.

"Yes?"

"Katherine Brewster?"

"Who's calling? Do you know what time it is?"

"Katherine Brewster, please. This is a veterinary emergency."

"She's not here. She's at the clinic. It's the same thing I told the guy who called five minutes ago."

T-X hung up.

Santa Clara

Strictly speaking, Terminator was incapable of experiencing human feelings, or of having premonitions. But he could and did constantly evaluate data: old data from his memory banks, and new data that his sensors continuously gathered. From such evaluations he could make predictive forecasts to which he could assign probability values.

He was programmed to know that Skynet was sending or had already sent back a terminator. He was also programmed with the knowledge that it was a T-X assigned to eliminate targets of opportunity, among them John Connor and Katherine Brewster.

Finally, he was programmed, by Connor himself, to understand that in this era Connor was what might be called a loose cannon; no permanent address and only scanty personal records in a few databases.

The T-X would understand this, and would probably view Katherine Brewster as a preliminary target.

Terminator's head-up display assigned an 88.97733451 percent probability to such a scenario.

After he had spoken with the man who answered Katherine Brewster's home telephone, Terminator increased the scenario probability to 94.5365555 percent.

From his database he brought up Katherine's place of employment, Emery Animal Hospital, pinpointed the address on a map of the Los Angeles area, and headed there.

Traffic was light at this hour of the morning, mostly semis. With his onboard electronic emissions detectors (which included radar) he pushed the truck to speeds in excess of one hundred miles per hour.

The Valley

Out in the lobby Kate saw who was ringing the front buzzer, and she groaned inwardly.

She was still in a state of shock that she recognized the guy she'd locked in the cage. But the more she thought about it the more worried she became. There'd been trouble around him.

Kate unlocked the front door, and Betsy Steinberg, one of Emery's regular and more obnoxious customers, pushed her way past with her pet carrier clutched firmly in her grip.

"It's Hercules, I think he's got pneumonia. He just started coughing and he wouldn't stop—" The woman was about Kate's age and general build, but she could be very insistent, something Kate normally wasn't.

"Betsy, I've got a problem in back."

"A problem?" the woman shouted, alarmed. "This is an emergency!"

Kate peered into the carrier. Hercules was a pampered, overfed, overweight Siamese cat whose only problem was his owner, who treated the cat like a person and not like an animal. The cat lowered its head and coughed politely.

"Sounds like a hairball," Kate said.

"I know what hairballs sound like," Betsy shrilled. "Where's Dr. Monroe?"

"It's five-thirty in the morning, I'm sure he's home sleeping. He'll come in if he has to—" Kate smiled, softening. The woman was frightened enough about the safety of an animal she obviously loved to get up and come down to the clinic. "Look, just wait here with Hercules. I'll be just a few minutes, all right?"

Betsy searched Kate's face to make sure that she wasn't being blown off, then nodded. "Okay."

Kate went back into the kennel, picked up the Torbutrol bottle, and hunched down in front of the cage that held her prisoner.

"Did you call the cops?" Connor asked.

"Not yet."

Connor glanced at the empty bottle. "Am I going to need my stomach pumped or something?"

Kate felt a little sorry for him. He looked forlorn. Lost. "You took a couple hundred milligrams of a narcotic . . . you're going to be out of it for a while. That's all."

Connor nodded.

"You're John Connor," Kate blurted.

A look of surprise flickered in his eyes.

"I'm Kate Brewster. West Hills Junior High."

Connor had to laugh quietly; there was nothing much else he could do under the circumstances. He shook his head. "Nice seeing you again, Kate."

■ ■ ■

T-X came around the corner past the Universal Rentals lot with the big yellow crane behind the fence, and pulled up behind a pickup truck and a Cadillac DeVille parked in front of the animal clinic.

The veterinary hospital was a match with T-X's files.

She got out of the Lexus and started up the walk.

"What happened to you, John?" Kate asked.

It was a good question, Connor thought. He lay back against the bars and closed his eyes. How to summarize his crazy life in twenty-five words or less?

"Middle of the eighth grade, you just disappeared. And there was something about your foster parents—"

"They were murdered," Connor replied, opening his eyes.

Kate reared back.

"I didn't do it," Connor said, matter-of-factly. How to explain that part to her? Impossible. "So, wow," he said, trying to lighten it up a bit. "West Hills. Those were the days." He grinned at her. "I don't suppose for old times' sake you'd just let me—"

Something crashed out front. Kate looked up, alarmed. It sounded like a lot of glass breaking. Almost as if a car or truck or something had crashed through the front windows.

She turned back to Connor. "What the hell—? Is somebody with you?"

Connor shook his head. "No."

Kate stood up and hurried into the hall to the reception area. She was just in time at the door to see Betsy come around the corner as a stunning-looking blond woman stepped through the smashed front door, a big gun in her hand.

The woman raised the pistol without a moment's hesitation and fired twice, both shots hitting Betsy in the chest, driving her backward off her feet, blood flying everywhere, her arms and legs splaying out.

Kate took a half step back away from the door, a scream caught in her throat. This wasn't happening. She couldn't move. She could not utter a sound as she watched in horror.

The blond walked to where Betsy lay and bent down over her.

"Katherine Brewster?"

Betsy was still alive. Her mouth moved, trying to form a word, but she could not speak.

The blond touched a delicate finger into the blood that covered Betsy's chest, then raised it to her lips.

A moment later the woman shook her head. "No," she said softly.

The dogs were barking furiously, howling and baying, knowing instinctively that death was nearby. Hercules the cat was out of his pet carrier. He sauntered around from behind the counter, glanced at his owner and then up at the blond woman, a look of indifference on the feline features.

Kate backed up as the woman turned and came directly toward her. It suddenly registered on her that the killer had used her name! She realized that she had just a second to make a decision; stay and be shot to death like Betsy, or move and try to live.

She turned and sprinted back into the storage room where she snatched her cell phone from the top of the file cabinet and ducked behind the stack of 'dog food boxes. With shaking hands she managed to enter 9 and then 1 before she fumbled the phone and it clattered to the floor.

Before she could retrieve it, the door opened and T-X stepped inside, the big gun sweeping left to right across the room.

The cell phone was on the floor less than a foot from the killer's right boot. Kate could do nothing but hold her breath.

T-X spotted the bloody gauze and other surgical supplies on the floor. She moved forward, picked up the gauze, and touched it to her tongue for a sample to process.

A double helix DNA sequence appeared in her head-up display. Lines of genetic code streamed across her eyes with lightning speed.

A moment later her head-up display cleared. John Connor's head shot came up over the legend: JOHN CONNOR—PRIMARY TARGET.

Kate watched with openmouthed amazement and fear. It was almost as if the killer had tasted the blood to see who it was from.

But that was crazy. This whole thing was insane. Surreal. It was a nightmare from hell.

Making as little noise as possible, Kate stepped out from behind the boxes, grabbed her keys, and dashed out the door back into the hallway.

The killer turned inhumanly fast, fired at the retreating figure, wood splinters hitting the back of Kate's neck, and continued to fire, emptying the gun as she gave chase.

Kate raced out into the reception area, skirting Betsy's blood-soaked body, her heart hammering nearly out of her chest.

The stupid cat leaped from out of nowhere, tangling with Kate's feet, sending her sprawling on all fours.

The cat howled in rage and pain and shot away as Kate picked herself up, ducked through the broken glass, and sprinted to the animal van.

This had something to do with John Connor. She'd had a bad feeling terrible things were going to happen the second she realized who he was. There had been a lot of weird shit going on when they were kids. It had been more than Connor's foster parents. There'd been other killings, explosions. Strange stuff.

His mother had even gone crazy and had been locked away. The rumor was that the woman claimed that robots from the future had come back to kill her.

Kate tore open the driver's side door, scrambled behind the wheel, locked the door, and fumbled to get the key in the ignition.

She looked up. The killer was right there! The homicidal woman ripped the driver's side door off its hinges. She tossed it aside as if it were nothing more than a piece of cardboard, and pulled Kate out of the truck, tossing her on the ground like a dishrag.

Kate frantically backpedaled, desperately trying to get away from the killer, but she jammed the heel of her boot into Kate's throat.

"Where is John Connor?"

Kate couldn't breathe, let alone speak. She managed to shake her head. Somewhere in the foggy distance she thought she heard the sound of a car or truck or something screeching around the corner at the end of the block, its engine revving high.

"He was here," the killer said in a calm, unhurried tone. "Where did he go?" She eased the pressure on Kate's neck.

Suddenly an impossibly large, dark presence loomed directly over Kate's head; screaming, roaring noise, the strong odors of burnt rubber, oil, gasoline, and something else, tall wheels bracketing her body.

The killer looked up at the same moment the grille of the big-wheeled Dodge pickup truck plowed into her body, carrying her in a seeming instant into the side of the Lexus convertible, bumping over the curb and shoving the entire mass of steel and plastic and cybernetic circuitry and framework into the side wall of the clinic.

For the briefest of moments the crash seemed to hang in midstride, until the leading edge of the wreck, still moving in excess of three meters per second, ruptured a large, three-fourths-full propane gas tank.

A huge ball of fire erupted, blowing straight up and then out, the heat instantly bringing tears to Kate's eyes.

Still dazed, she sat up as tremendous clouds of dust and black smoke billowed up from the great flash-bang of the explosion. She'd never seen anything like that in her life.

It was a pickup truck that had passed over her body, the wheels somehow miraculously missing her. She could see the back end of it sticking out of the wall.

She got unsteadily to her knees and rubbed her bruised neck where the killer's boot had been jammed into her throat.

She figured that the blond woman as well as whoever had been driving the pickup truck had to be dead. They could not have survived the crash and the fire. But something moved within the most intense area of flames.

Kate tried to shake herself out of her daze, unable to believe anything she was witnessing, unable even to believe her own rationality. She had to be dreaming, or hallucinating. Something.

This was not happening.

A tall man, wearing a leather jacket and trousers, boots on his feet, and a shotgun in his left hand, pushed through the jumbled mass of burning wreckage and melting steel and glass, shrugging out of the flames as if the heat and damage had absolutely no effect on him, and strode purposefully to Kate, who was frozen to the spot.

"Katherine Brewster," Terminator said as a statement of fact, not a question.

Kate could do nothing more than dumbly look up at him and nod.

The stranger scooped her up with his right arm, tossed her over his shoulder like a duffel bag, and brought her around to the back door of the animal van.

"Wait!" Kate shouted, coming out of her fog. "What are you doing?"

The tall man got the back door of the van open and he tossed her inside among a couple of empty animal cages, blankets, and some medical equipment. There were no windows in the pickup's cap. A security screen covered the sliding window into the cab.

"Where is John Connor?" the man asked, his tone neutral.

Kate didn't know what to say or do. "Look, if I tell you, you'll let me go, right?"

"Yes," he said.

"In the kennel. I locked him in one of the cages."

The man spotted a lug wrench attached to the spare-tire bracket. He pulled it free, and Kate shrank back, thinking he was going to hit her with it.

"You said you'd let me go!"

"I lied," he said, which strictly speaking was not true. In fact he had merely omitted the time frame. He would let her go, but not now.

He slammed the door, stuck the lug wrench through the latches, and without any apparent effort bent it into a steel loop, effectively locking Kate inside.

Terminator turned and strode toward the animal clinic's smashed front entrance, his processors evaluating the range of likely scenarios he was heading for.

■ ■ ■

Most of the fire was on the other side of the brick wall that separated the kennel from the rest of the building, but a big section of intersecting wall had collapsed in a heap of rubble, and the room was filling with smoke.

Connor kept smashing at the cage door with both feet, bracing himself against the rear bars with his back for more leverage.

The animals were howling and barking wildly. Like Connor they were frantic that they would burn to death or die of smoke inhalation before someone came to let them out.

One of the door hinges bent then broke. Connor savagely kicked the door one last time, and the second hinge broke, sending the door clattering to the floor.

He scrambled out of the cage, heedless of the wound to his leg. He wanted out of there right now. He started for the door, but then stopped and turned back. He couldn't leave.

The animals nervously switched their attention back and forth from him to the smoke pouring through the collapsed wall, almost pleading with him to help them.

"Shit," Connor muttered. He went back and started opening cages. The animals that could leaped out of their cages and raced for the door. Connor helped the others that were too sick to crawl out under their own steam. But once they were free and on the floor they were on their own.

He turned to get out of there when movement at the base of the rubble caught his eye. He stopped and watched as silver beads of liquid metal oozed out of the debris and began to pool on the concrete floor.

Connor stepped back a pace. He'd seen this kind of thing before. Twelve years ago. It was the T-1000 model that Skynet had sent back to kill him and his mother.

It was happening again.

"Oh, shit—"

A metallic arm coalesced from the liquid metal, and as even more material began to build on the first, clawlike structure, it was obvious that something very sophisticated was happening. This was no mere T-1000 rising out of the liquid metal.

This was something infinitely more deadly. Connor did not know how he knew such a thing, he just did.

He raced out of the kennel into the storage room where he retrieved his RAK PM-63 9mm machine pistol from where Kate had laid it, and headed out into the reception area, which was filled with dense smoke.

It was hard to breathe let alone see, and he nearly stumbled over the blood-soaked body of a woman.

At first he thought it was Kate, but then he heard the distinctive double click of a round being cycled into the breach of a shotgun. He stopped dead in his tracks, trying to figure his options before it was too late.

Terminator, the Mossberg 12-gauge 500 pump-action shotgun low at his right hip, appeared out of the smoke, reached Connor, grabbed him by the shirt, and lifted him up.

"John Connor," Terminator said. His head-up display

was slower and less sophisticated than the T-X's, but his processors came up with a very quick match. "It is time."

The first instance a T-800 had come back, it had been sent by Skynet to kill Connor's mother. The second T-800 had come to protect them. Now, twelve years later, it was anyone's guess what this unit—the newest model of the machine which had been the only father figure Connor had ever known—had been sent to do.

"You're here to kill me," Connor said.

"No," Terminator replied, perhaps a mild expression of surprise forming at the corners of his mouth and eyes. "You must live."

The Valley

Connor allowed himself to be hustled out of the clinic, partly because he knew there wasn't much he could do about it, and partly because of what was re-forming in the kennel.

"Why are you here?" he asked Terminator. "Where are we going?"

"Keep moving," Terminator said. He led Connor around to the back of the pet van and pushed him through the doorless driver's side. Fire still raged in the back of the building. Propane flames shot straight up into the dark, early morning sky. Debris littered the street.

In the distance, Connor thought he could hear a lot of sirens. Someone must have turned in the alarm. The cops and the fire department were on the way.

He glanced toward the front of the clinic in time to see T-X emerge through the shattered glass door.

"Shit. Look out!"

Terminator turned as T-X came toward them, the cyborg's liquid metal skin and clothing peeling back to reveal its formidable battle chassis armored with a crystalline ceramic that was interlaced with nano fibers of carbon and titanium. T-X's right arm had transformed into the same model of plasma weapon that had been used in Colorado to wipe out the commands of Colonel Earle and Lieutenant Benson. This was Skynet's latest.

Terminator stepped directly between the oncoming T-X and Connor and raised his shotgun.

"Get out of here," he told Connor.

He fired. The 12-bore slug plowed into T-X's armored skull, showing little effect other than opening a small liquid metal crater that immediately closed.

"Now!" Terminator insisted, firing a second time, and a third, and a fourth.

Connor finally got the van started and peeled away, tires screeching as Terminator headed directly for T-X, firing the last four shells.

He took more rounds that he'd found in the pickup truck from his jacket pocket and loaded them into the shotgun as an electric blue aura formed and intensified around T-X's plasma cannon.

A tremendous burst of raw energy, twenty-five or thirty millimeters in diameter, shot from the transmission head of the weapon, striking Terminator square in his broad chest.

He was not capable of feeling pain, but a firestorm raged across his battle-hardened neural networks, and a physical force as powerful as one hundred pounds of TNT picked him off his feet and propelled him across the street and through the front window of what appeared to be a hardware store. Glass and metal and bricks went flying as if a bomb had gone off just outside the store.

Terminator landed on his side on top of a pile of glass and tools from a display rack, his shotgun gone, his sunglasses askew. Blue plasma energy crackled through his body.

He was aware of his surroundings; aware of the still burning propane fire, of the approaching emergency vehicles, of his internal systems trying to reboot.

He was vulnerable now. Unable to perform his assigned duties.

Terminator hot-started many of his systems, shunting others, bringing as many battle and defensive subsystems on line as quickly as possible before T-X came to finish the job.

T-X turned in the direction that Connor had gone, but the pet van had already disappeared around the corner. A street map of the immediate area overlaid her head-up display. The probable paths that Connor could take increased exponentially with each elapsed minute.

She debated giving chase on foot—the T-X was capable of speeds in excess of eighty kilometers per hour for brief periods of time before its power packs began to show slight declines—or mounting a vehicular pursuit.

The solution presented itself as the first two squad cars and ambulances turned the corner at the end of the block, fire trucks and other emergency vehicles right behind them.

T-X evaluated the developing situation and moved up the street toward the equipment rental company as her flesh re-formed over the plasma cannon.

The first police officers to arrive immediately began taping off the entire area. Some of the paramedics rushed into the clinic, while others tried to get in close to the rear of the Dodge pickup that was still totally involved in the intense fire.

Two L.A. Fire Department pump units arrived, and their crews began setting up their equipment, while pairs of LAPD squad cars blocked off the intersections east and west.

People had materialized from somewhere, forming a small but growing crowd to watch what was happening.

T-X was just one person in the middle of the confusion. No one noticed her, not even the beefy fireman in all his gear who ran headlong into her, and bounced off as if he had run into a brick wall.

He picked himself up and ran off as T-X nonchalantly headed over to one of the unattended LAPD squad cars.

No one was watching as she lifted the hood, breaking the latch as if it were made of straw. She extended the data transfer point drill from her right index finger directly into the engine block.

In a matter of milliseconds she connected with the automobile's extremely crude but effective computers and reprogrammed them.

When she withdrew her finger and closed the hood, a blue glow lingered in the engine compartment.

■ ■ ■

In Kate's estimation, whatever John really wanted, he was at the very least a liar. She'd got that much from the few words he'd had with that creature she'd seen walking out of the middle of the flames.

God, this wasn't happening. She was still at home in bed having a bad dream. Any minute now Scott would nudge her shoulder. She would wake up suddenly and he would tell her that she was moaning in her sleep. She was having a nightmare.

Only she knew that she wasn't dreaming. She could still smell the fire. She could hear the man firing his shotgun at someone.

And the sirens. They seemed to come from every direction. They were much too loud for this to be a dream.

The pet van was bouncing all over the place, but Kate opened one of the emergency medical kits and found one of the clinic's cell phones. The battery was nearly dead, but she braced herself in a corner and managed to dial 911. It rang once.

A woman with a soothing voice answered. "This is nine-one-one. What is your emergency?"

"I'm being kidnapped," Kate said, her voice low but urgent.

"Yes, ma'am. Can you tell me where you are?"

"I don't know where. It's a Toyota pickup with a tan cap. It says Emery Animal Hospital on the side. I'm locked in the back."

The 911 operator didn't answer.

"Hello?" Kate said. "Hello?" She looked at the cell phone's display. The battery indicator showed discharged. "Shit," she said.

Connor figured that if he could make it to the freeway, he would have a good shot of getting out of the city. Out in the desert where he'd have some breathing room; time to figure out what the hell was going on.

But he wasn't familiar with this part of L.A., and he hadn't paid any attention earlier this morning when he'd caught the ride with the Mexicans. So he was driving blind. Sooner or later he'd have to cross one of the freeways though. It was an unavoidable fact of life in the city.

He just had to get that far.

Someone, or something, banged on the cab's rear window, and Connor nearly jumped out of his skin, almost smashing into a row of parked cars. They were still in a commercial section of the city: warehouses, hardware stores, appliance repair shops, air-conditioning shops.

He glanced over his shoulder. The window was painted black and it was protected by a heavy mesh screen. Whoever was back there banged on the window again.

Connor slid it open, and Kate was there.

"Let me out!" she screeched.

For a moment he didn't know what to say or do. He had no earthly idea how she had gotten into the back of the truck. He thought she was dead, back in the animal clinic.

"What the—what are you doing back there?"

"You tell me!" Kate shouted. "You got me into this!" She searched for words. Frustrated, angry, frightened. "That woman shot Betsy—the man, that man came out of the fire. Who *are* these people?"

"They're not people," Connor said. He felt truly sorry for her. She seemed like a nice person, although he couldn't remember her from West Hills. But that was a long time ago. A lot of things had happened since then. And somehow she had gotten into the middle of it.

"Stop the car!"

"I can't," Connor said. "Not yet."

"You can't keep me in here!" Kate screamed. She changed her tack. "Stop the car—please. Stop the car."

"Be quiet—"

She exploded. "You bastard! Stop the car!"

"Shut up," Connor shouted back. He reached over his shoulder to slide the partition shut, taking his eyes off the street just for a second.

A black Mercedes C280 came around the corner as Connor missed the stop sign and plowed into its rear end, sending them both to the side of the street.

Connor was shoved up against the steering wheel by the force of the impact, and Kate crashed into the front of the cap.

The accident wasn't serious, but the pet van had stalled and Kate was shouting for help.

The Mercedes's driver, a middle-aged man wearing jeans and a light pullover, jumped out to see how bad his car was damaged.

Connor opened the partition. "Are you okay back there? Are you hurt?"

"Let me out! Now!"

Connor tried to restart the pet van when the Mercedes's driver suddenly looked up.

"Goddammit," the man shouted. He was pissed off.

Connor continued trying to start the pet van.

"Hey, you!" the Mercedes's driver shouted, and he started back.

The Valley

LAFD paramedic Logan Ballinger had expected to see more bodies when the call came in. The explosion was a big one, and the fire would probably burn for quite a while before it was brought under control. Propane-fed fires were always a bitch.

But so far the only body was the guy in black leathers who'd apparently been blown right through the window of a hardware store.

He crunched through the glass and debris and set his emergency response kit next to the victim who was unconscious and apparently not breathing.

His partner, Eric Kraus, was right behind him.

Ballinger knelt down next to the man and touched a finger to the carotid artery in the side of his neck. There was no blood, or any obvious trauma, but the guy was as stiff as a board.

"No pulse," he said.

Kraus moved to the victim's opposite side as he pulled on surgical gloves. He opened a plastic sterile wrap and pulled out the CPR mask. "Turn him over."

Ballinger took the guy's shoulder and tried to ease him gently over on his back, but the man wouldn't budge. He was stiff. Some kind of paralysis, or maybe even rigor mortis already. He could have been here before the explosion.

"I can't," Ballinger said. "This guy weighs a ton."

T-X closed the sharply sloping hood of the ambulance she'd reprogrammed, a blue haze in the engine compartment.

The animal clinic was fully engulfed in fire now. Paramedics were bringing out the body of the woman from the reception room on a gurney.

It was obvious that the police were agitated because of the gunshot wounds in the woman's chest.

Soon they would try to completely seal off the area and question anyone they could round up. T-X wasn't concerned that such an action would stop her, but they might just slow her down.

Time just now was precious. With every moment that passed finding and eliminating John Connor became more and more problematic.

T-X evaluated her chances of finding Connor based on the continuously expanding time frame that gave him choices, and the likely pursuit of herself by the authorities once she moved out.

She walked over to another unattended LAPD radio car, opened its hood, and reprogrammed its computers, including those for the fuel, ignition, power steering, and automatic braking systems.

Next, she reprogrammed one more of the half dozen ambulances that had arrived to rescue the expected victims of such a large fire.

Radio cars and ambulances could be stopped by any number of conventional means at the disposal of the various police units on-site.

She needed something larger. Something so large that she would not have the inconvenience of being stopped and having to change vehicles.

She scanned the ground transport units available in the immediate vicinity, her eyes lighting on the huge mobile crane parked behind the National Rentals security fence. The word CHAMPION was painted in blue on its yellow boom that was telescoped over the cab of its massive blue tractor.

T-X brought up a file on the machine. It was a hydraulic truck crane weighing more than fifty metric tons, capable of making eighty kilometers per hour, fast enough so that the police couldn't stop it.

She skirted the rows of emergency vehicles and briskly walked to a service gate in the security fence.

The police were busy with crowd control, and the firemen were intent on battling the nasty blaze. No one noticed as T-X twisted the padlock off the gate and slipped inside. The shadows were deep in the storage yard, and it was not likely that she would be spotted and challenged.

She trailed her fingers along the truck's enormous

front bumper, her head-up display overlaid with the electronic and mechanical schematics for the truck as well as the crane's separate control. The truck was driven as a normal semi from the front cab. But the crane's functions were controlled from a computerized console at the rear.

She went around to the back, climbed up to the control platform, and for a few milliseconds studied the pedals, levers, and indicators, which she optically registered as a match with her head-up display.

She drilled a small hole directly into the control panel, and moments later transferred a stream of data from her system into the crane's computer.

When she withdrew her data transfer probe, a soft blue haze played in and around the crane's controls like a delicate fog backlit by a blue neon sign.

The sky was beginning to get light with the dawn as T-X climbed down from the crane, walked to the front of the cab, and climbed up behind the wheel of the tractor.

She studied the driving controls, which, except for the transmission levers, were not much different from those of a police vehicle.

She brought up twin overlays in her head-up display. To the left she studied a street map, and to the right were four rows of symbols. Two controlled the pair of ambulances she had reprogrammed, and two the pair of police cars. From this point she was in ultra-high frequency contact with each of the vehicles via a downlink with a military communications satellite 22,500 miles out in a geosynchronous orbit over the Pacific Ocean that already was coming under Skynet control.

She drilled into the truck's steering column next to the ignition switch, transferred a few hundred bytes of data, and the truck's engine roared to life.

Simultaneously, the engines in the two ambulances and two police cars revved up.

Terminator's eyes suddenly opened and he looked up at a very startled Logan Ballinger, who reared back as did his partner, Eric Kraus.

The man was dead. Now he was alive. They'd heard about stuff like this, but they'd never seen it.

"I must go," Terminator said. He sat up, straightened his sunglasses, got to his feet, and strode out of the hardware store, leaving the two paramedics with their mouths hanging open.

On the street, Terminator picked up the shotgun from where he'd dropped it, and optically catalogued the current situation.

Police and fire units were busy at work, as were paramedics emerging from the clinic with sick and injured animals in their arms.

A crowd had gathered beyond the police barriers, but there was no sign of either John Connor and Kate Brewster, or of the T-X.

More sirens were converging on the scene as Terminator processed the available data overlaid with probable scenarios and suggested courses of action.

John Connor and Kate Brewster were gone. The T-X would pursue them. It was only a matter of finding one or the other.

Which suddenly happened.

Two police cars and two ambulances roared to life and peeled out in the same direction Connor had gone with the pet van. But no one was driving.

Cops and firemen scattered out of the way.

A police officer ran up to one of the squad cars, and made a desperate grab for the steering wheel, but he was thrown clear as the unit burned rubber accelerating.

Terminator's onboard electronic emissions detector immediately pinpointed downlink signals to the four emergency vehicles, but he was not capable of tracking the source to the specific transmitting satellite.

A powerful diesel engine roared to life, and Terminator turned in time to see the huge Champion crane leap forward, crashing through the chain-link fence.

It turned ponderously in the same direction as the police units and ambulances had gone, emergency personnel scrambling to get out of its way.

As it accelerated up the street, Terminator caught a brief glimpse of the T-X behind the wheel. He deduced from available information that she had sent the radio cars and ambulances out as scouts to track John Connor and Kate Brewster.

He would follow the T-X.

Terminator stepped out into the middle of the street

as a motorcycle cop came around the corner, followed by another fire engine.

The cop tried to avoid a collision, but Terminator grabbed the bike's handlebars and swung it around like a toy.

"I'll drive," he said as the cop skidded across the street on his back.

The motorcycle was an Indian, with a windscreen and wind deflector. Capable of speeds in excess of 130 miles per hour, it would do the job.

In one smooth motion Terminator stashed his shotgun in the saddle rack, hopped aboard, and hammered the throttle to its stop as he downshifted into second.

The motorcycle took off as if it were shot from a cannon as the mobile crane, still gathering speed, lumbered around the corner at the end of the block.

The Valley

In the back of the pet van Kate was desperately trying to pry open the rear door, but the latch was jammed.

They'd hit something and Connor had stopped. She could hear a man shouting. He sounded very angry.

"You did something to the doors," she screamed at Connor. "I can't get the back open."

The man said something else she couldn't quite make out. But it sounded like he was closer than before. Right in front of the van.

"Help!" Kate shouted. "Let me out of here. Help!"

"What's going on?" the man shouted, and Kate could hear him plainly now. He was just a few feet away. "What are you doing?" he demanded.

"I'm being kidnapped," Kate screamed. "Call the police. Call nine-one-one."

The man was right next to the driver's side. "What? Who's there?"

"Help me!"

Connor was trying to start the pickup truck's engine but it didn't want to catch.

"Where do you think you're going?" the Mercedes's driver yelled. "Hey! I'm talking to you! Get out of there!"

"Help! Let me out of here," Kate cried. "For God's sake, someone please help me."

"What's going on in there?" the Mercedes's driver demanded. He thumped the side of the van. "What are you doing?"

The pet van's engine suddenly roared into life. Connor threw it into reverse and the pickup careened away from the Mercedes.

"Hey!" the driver shouted. "Get back here!"

Kate was thrown against the rear door as Connor dropped the pickup into drive and jammed the gas pedal to the floor.

"Oh, God," Kate cried weakly. It was never going to end. "Oh, God—help me."

In Connor's estimation they had spent way too much time screwing around at the accident scene. Unless he missed his guess, that machine at the clinic was something new, and Terminator wasn't going to have an easy time with it.

One thing he was absolutely sure of, however, was that the new cyborg would not stop coming after him until he was dead, or it was destroyed.

He had been down this path before. There were no other options.

The only question in his mind was how the hell the

new machine, and Terminator, had traced him to the animal clinic. That part wasn't making any sense to him.

Kate pounded on the rear window. "You can't do this to me!" she raged. "Pull over and let me out. Now!"

Connor reached over his shoulder and slid the window open. "I can't let you out. You're just going to have to trust me."

"Yeah, right," Kate said. She was totally frazzled, at her wits' end, frightened.

Traffic was starting to pick up with delivery trucks and workmen making their sleepy way to early shifts. Connor had to dodge in and around the slower traffic, while all the while he kept checking his rearview mirror.

At any moment he expected to see something behind him. The cyborg would be coming. He would be willing to bet money on it.

A big ball of flame and black smoke rose in the sky around the corner a couple of blocks behind him, and Connor's gut tightened. It was happening faster than he'd feared it would.

Suddenly he could hear sirens. He glanced in his rearview mirror again in time to see a pair of black-and-whites screeching around the corner, lights flashing.

If the cyborg caught up with him and Kate, it would not hesitate to kill them on the spot. But if they were stopped by the cops, arrested and tossed in a holding cell, the end result would be the same. The machine would track them down and kill them.

"That's the cops," Kate shouted over his right shoulder. "Now you'll have to pull over."

"Yeah, first chance I get," Connor said. He pulled around a slow-moving UPS truck and jammed the gas pedal to the floor.

They were still in a commercial section of the city, lots of warehouses, big buildings, shops, and parts stores.

"What? You think you can get away from them? Are you crazy?"

The first of the two cop cars was right on Connor's tail. It pulled up beside him, and he glanced over, nearly losing control of the pet van and running it up onto the curb.

No one was driving the squad car. There was no one behind the wheel. No one in the passenger seat, or in the rear. The car was driving itself.

The black-and-white swerved right, slamming into the side of the pet van. Connor had just time enough to lean out of the way as part of the squad car's door entered the pet van's cab. He hauled the pickup truck hard to the right, just missing a pair of parked cars, bumped over the curb and up onto the sidewalk, the van's shocks bottoming out with a bone-jarring bang.

The second squad car roared up on the sidewalk behind him, smashing into his right rear fender, metal crunching, glass and plastic breaking.

Connor had just a split second to see that no one was driving this cop car either, before he skidded over the curb and back out onto the street. The pet van's left front tire dug in, nearly causing them to flip over, before he regained control.

This was nuts. But he knew damned well it was something that the new machine was somehow orchestrating. He'd seen this kind of weird shit before.

Something else crashed into the rear of the pet van, this time one of a pair of ambulances, lights flashing, sirens blaring. Connor didn't have to look to know that neither of them had a driver behind the wheel.

He just hoped that Kate was somehow okay in the back.

Abruptly the ambulances dropped back. Connor hauled the pet van around a corner and stomped on the gas pedal.

"Hold on back there," he shouted to Kate.

Terminator hung a few meters off the Champion crane's left rear bumper. The ponderous machine thundered like an express train down city streets, taking out cars, trucks, and anything else in its path.

Moments ago the T-X had crushed a car, its gas tank igniting with a big ball of flame and black smoke. Terminator barely avoided the fireball.

He could see the T-X's reflection in the broad driver's side mirror. She turned and spotted him, their eyes locking for an instant. Terminator registered an extremely brief dilation of the T-X's pupils, indicating a mild form of what could be classified as AI surprise.

The T-X had expected that he had been destroyed in front of the animal clinic.

It was a mistake. The T-X was not infallible after all.

The pair of driverless ambulances dropped back in front of the crane, like a shark's remora, and then slid back along either side of the big machine.

Suddenly the Champion's huge boom lifted off its cradle and began to extend, while rotating to the left.

The ambulances dropped back on either side of Terminator, then swerved inward, trying to crush him between them.

At the last possible moment, Terminator slammed on the bike's front brake. The rear tire lifted high off the pavement, but the Indian stopped nearly in its tracks, just managing to clear the rear bumpers of the two ambulances as they crashed together.

The crane's boom continued to extend and swing around, taking out electric wires and transformers above the street in showers of sparks.

Terminator grabbed his shotgun. When the ambulances separated, he hammered the throttle, pulling a wheelie. He roared between them, firing over his left shoulder at the nearest ambulance, taking out one of its front tires.

It dropped back, but did not drop out.

The Champion crane surged forward.

Behind T-X was the T-850 that Skynet expected the human resistance would send back, along with the two ambulances that were working the problem.

She was helping that element by using the extended

boom to lay down a continuous debris path that might slow the obsolete model warrior/cyborg.

Ahead of her was the target, John Connor. His van was damaged, and she could sense the heat signature of an overworked engine that was leaking lubricating oil from a rear seal in the aft section of the main mass of the block.

Two LAPD remote units were harrying Connor, but to this point they had not been completely effective. The human showed the unusually strong resilience and inventiveness that Skynet had programmed her to expect.

T-X punched a hole in the windshield, morphed her right arm into her plasma weapon, and quickly charged the unit.

Her head-up unit displayed a reticle roughly centered on the pet van. Her target-acquisition stabilizing circuitry popped up and the reticle locked on the pickup truck.

Her weapon indicator showed fully charged as the pet van and flanking police cars raced through a red light, just avoiding collisions with two automobiles.

T-X fired at the same instant a semi tractor-trailer entered the intersection, filling her targeting frame.

For an instant nothing seemed to happen. But then the semi was engulfed in a blue plasma charge field and exploded with an impressive flash-bang that sent flames and debris hammering off the fronts of the commercial buildings on either side of the street.

The Champion crane plowed through the debris like a hot knife through soft butter, and on the other side, T-X glanced in her rearview mirror.

Terminator, his motorcycle laid over on its side, skidded through the flames, then shot upright, apparently unharmed.

Behind it, the first ambulance ran headlong into a major piece of the semi's frame and disintegrated, while the second ambulance emerged from the fire, leaving behind twin vortex swirls in the dense smoke.

A huge explosion obliterated the intersection behind Connor. He looked in his rearview mirror in time to see the Champion crane crash through the fire and debris, followed a second later by Terminator on the police bike, and one of the ambulances directly on his tail.

It was Terminator! Somehow he had caught up.

They weren't out of the woods yet, but Connor felt a small measure of relief. He and Kate were no longer alone. Terminator might be an older model of cyborg, but he'd been there in the past for John, and it looked as if he would be there again.

For the briefest of instants, Connor wished that his mother were here. But then he put that thought out of his mind.

First, he would have to survive this trouble.

The driverless cop cars still flanked him. And it wouldn't take much more for them to finally box the pet van in and run it off the street.

"Hold on," he shouted to Kate in the back.

He slammed the brake pedal as hard as he could,

locking up the pet van's wheels, smoke pouring off the tires.

The cop cars shot past, and Connor made a sloppy but effective four-wheel drift to the right, just missing a delivery truck at the corner.

The pair of cop cars locked up their brakes in unison and made perfect 180s, jumping back on Connor's tail as quickly as they'd been thrown off.

The Champion crane took the corner wide, the extended boom taking out the entire side of a building, brick and wood and plastic exploding in every direction.

Whatever kind of weapon the cyborg had fired had been big enough to take out an entire semi truck. One hit, even a near miss, would make short work of the pet van.

Connor kept checking the rearview mirror as the huge crane actually gained on him, rolling over cars whose drivers weren't quick enough to get out of the way, whereas he could only weave in and out of the slower-moving traffic.

But the ambulance and Terminator were still back there, along with the cop cars in some kind of a crazy Fourth of July parade complete with fireworks.

There was a large hole in the Champion crane's windshield and something jutted out from inside.

Connor swerved hard to the right, nearly sideswiping a row of parked cars, and then swerved sharply left, laying on his horn for cars to get out of his way.

Kate was being thrown from side to side in the back. He could hear her body slamming against the cap.

"Stop it!" she screamed in desperation. "Stop it!"

But he could not. Their lives depended on his driving.

He could see a bright blue glow around whatever it was sticking out of the crane's windshield. It was the cyborg's weapon. And it was ready to fire again.

The Valley

Terminator could see the blue glow in the cab of the Champion crane as the T-X made ready to fire a second time.

Ahead, Connor was maneuvering wildly, but that would not work for long. The police cars would box him in and T-X would destroy him and Kate.

Terminator took the Mossberg from the saddle rack, cycled a round into the breech, and fired at the crane's left rear tire. The machine had eighteen wheels, but the one shredding tire was enough to cause T-X to lurch a little to the side at the same moment she fired.

The shot went wild. The beam of raw energy struck the rear of the squad car off Connor's right, instantly incinerating it. The flaming wreckage tumbled end over end.

Terminator prepared to take a second shot when the ambulance behind him jolted his rear tire, almost making him lose the bike.

The crane's boom accelerated to the left as it extended, dropping a massive hook on thick cables that swung like a lethal wrecking ball.

The hook smashed into Terminator's chest, slamming him off the motorcyle. At the last moment he grabbed on to it with one hand, still holding the shotgun in the other.

Suddenly he was swinging wildly to the left. He twisted his body just as he slammed hard into the pursuing ambulance, shoving it over on its side, sending it skidding down the street in a trail of sparks.

Terminator swung right again in time to see Connor, still harried by one of the squad cars, duck down a side street and disappear.

It was too sharp a turn for the crane, which roared through the intersection. Terminator, dangling from the hook, smashed off parked cars, lampposts, and anything else in his path as he continued to try to bring his shotgun to bear on the T-X's head.

The crane suddenly swerved to the right, crashed over two parked cars, jumped the sidewalk, and smashed into the glass wall of a building.

Terminator found himself crashing into pieces of brick and steel and wires and pipes and girders as the massive machine careened down a long work area and burst through the opposite wall, back out onto the street in the next block.

As the big crane made the impossibly sharp right turn with the boom extended, carrying Terminator's two hundred kilos out at ninety degrees, it lifted off the nine wheels on the left, balanced there, ponderously, like a huge whale about to be beached by a gigantic comber, but then regained its balance when the front end finally came around.

Connor was on the next street over, and Terminator's head-up overlay map of the local streets showed that the pet van would have to come down this street. T-X had the same overlay.

Terminator twisted around and brought his shotgun to bear directly on the T-X's cranial case, hoping to at least take out its optical lenses, when something large, horns and sirens blaring, loomed directly in front of him.

He turned at the same instant a mammoth hook and ladder fire truck, moving at high speed, struck him square in the torso. The force of the collision was so great he lost his grip on the crane's hook, which went flying upward to the right, and his shotgun, which arched overhead to his left.

The Champion crane flashed away.

Terminator felt the much weaker metal and glass of the fire truck collapse under his weight. The entire machine shuddered from front to rear, two massive motor mounts on its Cummins diesel snapped like dry twigs. Ladders broke loose and lights shattered under the sheer mechanical shock wave that coursed through the truck's frame.

Terminator's head and upper torso passed through the shattered windshield, and he found himself, one hand on the big steering wheel, looking up at two firemen, shocked beyond movement, mindless of the blood streaming from the cuts on their faces from the flying glass. What they were witnessing simply could not be happening.

"I'll drive," Terminator said.

Both firemen came to life at the same moment. They shoved open the doors and bailed out, hitting the street and tumbling end over end, protected by their helmets and heavy fire suits from any serious injuries.

Terminator, still holding the wheel, climbed into the cab of the rapidly decelerating fire truck, studied the controls for just a moment, then jammed the gas pedal to the floor as he prepared to make a 180.

Connor had managed to shake the big crane, but he'd also lost Terminator at the last turn. The one cop car was still on his tail, repeatedly smashing into the Toyota's rear fender, trying to spin him out.

The temperature gauge on the panel was just about in the red and the fuel tank was getting low, but other than that he figured his luck was holding so far. Some luck, he thought.

"Kate, are you okay?" he shouted over his shoulder.

The cop car came up on his left side again, edging closer. It was almost as if the driverless squad car was trying to herd him.

"What do you think?" Kate shouted angrily.

The squad car *was* trying to herd him.

Connor made a sharp right turn, then left again, coming back out onto the main avenue through the industrial district.

The Champion crane was there. Less than fifty yards

down the street, barreling right at him. Its boom was extended forward and its hook was throwing up showers of sparks as it tumbled and banged along the road.

Connor slammed the gas to the floor, but the squad car pulled ahead and swerved directly into his path. He had to hit the brakes.

He hauled the pet van left and tried to get around the cop car, but he was cut off again.

The crane halved the distance between them, and T-X recharged her weapon for a final shot that could not miss at this range.

Terminator pulled up alongside the Champion crane.

The T-X was preparing to fire again.

Terminator knew that she could not possibly miss at this range. Even if he could somehow shove the crane aside at the moment the T-X fired, she would fire again and again until she succeeded. Or, at the very least, she would simply run over the pet van, crushing John Connor and Katherine Brewster to death.

The T-X had to be stopped.

Terminator found the control for the fire truck's stabilizers and activated it. The thick metal arms, which were meant to provide a broad footing for the truck when its ladder and basket were deployed, extended from the bottom of the truck's high chassis.

When they were nearly fully deployed, Terminator hauled the fire truck hard to the right. The stabilizers bit into the eight remaining tires on the crane's left side, chewing them apart like office paper through a shredding machine.

The crane swerved to the right, almost impossible even for the T-X to maintain a straight track.

Terminator pulled away and immediately hauled the fire truck back toward the crane, hoping to knock the big machine over the curb and onto its side.

The Champion's much larger stabilizers deployed at that moment, slashing into the side of the fire truck in two places, the thick metal arms impaling the hook and ladder unit, lifting it partially off its wheels.

Terminator now had no control over the fire truck, but neither did the T-X have much control over the combined mass of both machines.

He looked up in time to see T-X point her fully charged plasma cannon at him.

The cab of the fire truck disintegrated in a blue flash, molten metal and glass bursting outward as if the truck had been a mass of mercury dropped onto the pavement.

T-X found that she still had enough control of the Champion crane to complete this element of the mission. In fact, the fire truck attached to her left side acted like an outrigger.

The Emery pet van was less than ten meters ahead, just out of the range of the dangling hook, but still effectively boxed in by the squad car.

All other traffic on the road had pulled out of the way. It wouldn't be long before the LAPD arrived in force. Already the 911 switchboard was being flooded with calls, even more not getting through because of computer problems at Pacific Bell's main L.A. exchange.

T-X waited indifferently for her weapon to recharge.

As the power cell came into the green range, she aimed the weapon at the back of the van, her target-acquisition stabilizing system switching to active.

Terminator, his chest smoking from where his torso had caught the edge of the plasma beam before he could get out of the cab and the bare metal of his cranial case exposed where the patches of flesh on his face had been seared away, grabbed a fire axe from its bracket in the back.

The T-X was getting ready to fire again. The blue plasma glow was rapidly intensifying.

Terminator scrambled up on the fire truck's ladder basket and swung over the top of the Champion's cab, the roof sagging under his weight.

He stepped back, balancing on the edge, as the sheet metal was blasted from inside, and the T-X burst up through the blue-tinged opening, moving like some predatory creature out of its lair ready for a battle to the death.

Terminator was waiting. He swung the fire axe with every kilo of his T-850 chassis's strength at the cyborg's skull as she rose up out of the cab.

The axe blade bit into the first layers of the T-X's

cranial case, but immediately struck the malleable ceramic/titanium armor. The axe handle shattered, and although no vital circuits had been damaged, the force of the blow was enough to sweep the T-X off the roof of the crane, and down between the two vehicles locked together as they barreled down the street.

Terminator dropped down into the Champion's cab. The T-X had taken control of the throttle, so despite the unstable condition of the damaged fire truck and the shredded wheels on the left side of the crane, they were actually gaining on the pet van, which was very close now.

He angled the rearview mirror down so he could see what was going on between the fire truck and crane. The T-X was pulling herself up from one of the stabilizers, her plasma cannon charging again.

Time was running short. If the T-X incapacitated him again the way she had in front of the animal clinic, she would be free to destroy John Connor and Katherine Brewster.

He could not allow that to happen.

He was about to steer the crane into the brick wall of a building when his optical system spotted road hazard sawhorses in the middle of the street about fifty meters ahead. Traffic was meant to maneuver around some kind of an obstacle.

He enhanced his optical circuits momentarily. The obstacle was an open manhole. The steel cover was lying to one side.

Connor, behind the squad car, did not spot the barricades in time to avoid them. But he did manage to miss the open manhole by inches. The pet van fishtailed nearly out of control down the street.

The cop car spun out and stalled at the same time Terminator hauled the Champion's steering wheel hard right, then left, then right again.

The big hook, bouncing and skipping up the street at the end of the extended boom, swung left and then right like a pendulum. It just caught the edge of the open manhole and dropped down inside the tunnel, the thick steel cables unreeling like a fishing line that had snagged a whale.

Terminator pulled himself back up on the roof of the cab as the hook caught on something solid.

The cable suddenly went taut as Terminator leaped from the Champion crane onto the roof of the pet van.

He swung himself over the side through the open driver's door, shoving Connor aside.

"Hold on," he said, and he stamped the gas pedal to the floor.

He swung around the cop car and glanced in the rearview mirror in time to see the entire tangled mass of the Champion crane and the LAFD truck, between which T-X was preparing to take her shot, stop dead in the street as the front of the boom dug into the pavement.

The back of the wreck shot straight up into the air, the eighty or ninety combined tons of metal and glass and plastic coming down like an earth-shattering meteor on the squad car, instantly flattening it. The entire mass erupted in a huge ball of fire, the blast shattering windows along the entire city block.

North of Los Angeles

Terminator divided his primary action circuits between driving and checking his rearview mirror and electronic emissions detectors for any signs that they were being followed.

He wanted to get out of the city as soon as possible, but not via the main highways or the more heavily traveled county roads. In the condition the pet van was in they would attract too much attention. They did not have time for diversions.

He also understood that the T-X had not been destroyed in the crash. That chassis was extremely battle-hardened. It would probably take more than the crash of even something as large as the Champion crane with its attendant explosion and fire to destroy the cyborg.

Which meant that T-X would continue to follow them, acting on her prime directive, that of assassinating John Connor and Katherine Brewster.

But there was even more at stake than just their lives.

They were finally out of the industrial areas of the

city, and they got on a two-lane highway that led up into the hills.

Safe, Terminator thought. He was not able to detect anyone behind them, nor was he picking up the satellite downlink signals that the T-X had used to control the emergency vehicles that had nearly cost Connor and Kate their lives.

Safe, Terminator thought again. But only temporarily.

He turned to look at John Connor, who'd been staring at him since their narrow escape. He reached out and gently touched Connor's face, raising one eyelid and then the other, his optical sensors set on magnify.

"No sign of brain trauma," Terminator said.

Connor pulled his head away. "Yeah, I'm fine. Thanks."

Terminator glanced at the highway. Traffic was slowly starting to pick up as people headed for work. It was a Saturday, otherwise there would be many more vehicles on the road.

Originally, the T-800 series warrior/cyborgs had been programmed to do battle primarily with other robotic units, and human soldiers from enemy states. After Judgment Day, Skynet reprogrammed most of them to hunt and kill any and all humans. His particular unit had been upgraded to a T-850 and programmed to act as a human infiltration model with one mission: preserve the lives of John Connor and Katherine Brewster.

That was his prime directive.

He neither liked nor disliked humans, Connor included. But he was programmed to protect them, and to understand their motivations well enough to help predict how they might act under any given set of circumstances.

Humans were, in his estimation, highly irrational organisms. Their directives were continually being influenced, most often for the worse, by emotional considerations: love, hate, envy, jealousy, fear. And many others. In Terminator's main memory he had access to a file with more than one thousand different emotional elements that modified human behavior. And that, his file cautioned, was only a partial list.

Compounding the difficulty was the phenomenon of multitasking; humans were almost always motivated by more than one emotion. Sometimes by a multitude of them, each subtly acting upon the others in an endless series of combinations.

Starting with the one thousand elements in Terminator's files, he could come up with something in excess of 8×10^9, or eight billion, combinations.

It was no wonder, he continued in the evaluation process, that even for humans the job of understanding each other was often next to impossible.

"Do you even remember me?" Connor asked.

Terminator glanced at him, but made no reply.

"Sarah Connor? Blowing up Cyberdyne? '*Hasta la vista,* baby.' Ring any bells?"

"That was an old model T-800," Terminator said, which was technically true. That had been a different *chassis.*

Connor looked away momentarily, and shook his head. It seemed as if he felt the weight of the world on his shoulders. "So, what—?" he asked. He looked at Terminator. "You guys come off an assembly line, or something?"

"Or something. I'm a new model. A T-850."

Connor was less disappointed than he was bemused. "Oh, man. I gotta teach you everything all over again."

Terminator looked over his shoulder through the dividing window. "Katherine Brewster. Have you sustained injury?"

Kate came to the screen. Blood trickled from the corner of her mouth where she'd bitten her lip. Her hair was a mess, and the rear of the pet van was in complete disarray. She looked as if she'd been through the spin cycle of a washing machine.

"Drop dead, asshole," she told him.

Terminator closed the window. "I am unable to comply," he said.

The Valley

Sirens converged, it seemed, from all over the city of Los Angeles on the mangled, burning wreckage of the National Rentals' Champion crane, the LAFD hook and ladder unit, and the LAPD squad car.

People were already gathering closer to the scene of the accident, drawn to the flames like moths.

Someone had to have been killed. No one could have survived. There was wreckage strewn along a five-block area. There had to be bodies, though a few of the spectators had witnessed what they thought was a man leaping from the crane just before it crashed. But nobody was going to believe that.

A high-pitched whine came from deep inside the tangled mass of metal. People stepped back. There was no telling what dangerous chemicals were in there.

At the base of the fire truck's chassis a gap appeared that widened as if someone or something was opening a tent flap.

T-X, her left hand formed into a diamond-toothed metal saw, stepped out of the wreckage. She glanced with indifference at the small crowd, then walked away, her hand morphing back into human form, her skin and clothing in perfect condition. Not so much as a strand of hair out of place.

No one tried to stop her, or even talk to her.

Around the corner in the next block, she hot-wired a blue Saturn and headed back into the city. Her head-up display was overlaid with a street map on which was pinpointed the home address of Katherine Brewster.

The Foothills

The Toyota's temperature gauge hovered just below the red mark and the needle on the gas gauge bounced half-way between ¼ and E.

Terminator's head-up display showed a map of the countryside in the hills above Los Angeles. Most highways eventually led over the mountains down into the Mojave Desert. He had a destination, but there was little value in informing either John Connor or Katherine Brewster at this time.

They would be told what they needed to know, when they needed to know it.

Something crashed in the back. Connor turned and looked through the dividing window. Kate was kicking at the back door, trying to force it off its hinges, or to break free whatever was holding it shut.

He'd almost forgotten about her. He turned back to Terminator. "Get off the highway as soon as you can. We have to let her out."

Terminator glanced at him. "Negative. Katherine Brewster must be protected."

"Why—?"

A curl of acrid smoke rose from Terminator's chest. He looked at it. His internal diagnostic programs had warned him that one of his fuel cells was going critical. But the rate of failure was evidently accelerating. "I require a cutting tool," he said.

Connor looked doubtfully at the smoke, but he handed Terminator his Gerber from his belt pouch. "I thought I was the one they're after."

Terminator opened the utility tool and studied the longest blade for a moment. "You could not be located, so a T-X was sent back through time to eliminate others who could become enemies of Skynet. Your lieutenants."

Connor glanced at Kate in the back. She was huddled now in the far corner by the door, her knees up to her chin, a sullen look on her round, pretty face.

"So, she's going to be in the resistance—" he started. But that didn't make any sense. Judgment Day had never come. "But if—No, no." He looked at Terminator, trying to gauge the cyborg's meaning by the look on his face. Which was futile.

Terminator waited patiently for Connor to work it out.

"You shouldn't even exist. We took out Cyberdyne over ten years ago."

"Cyberdyne backed up its research data," Terminator explained. "They saved it off-site. When the company went bankrupt in 1993, Cyber Research Systems acquired the assets and developed the technology in secret."

"But we *stopped* Judgment Day," Connor insisted. He'd lived with that knowledge for the past twelve years.

"You only postponed it. Judgment Day is inevitable."

Connor sat back, defeated. There was no defense against this kind of circular logic. As he'd been from the beginning, he was nothing more than a pawn between the machines and humans in some future war. And time travel made anything possible.

Or, perhaps, *impossible*.

"Take the wheel," Terminator ordered.

Connor snapped out of his thoughts and he grabbed the steering wheel as Terminator, his foot still on the gas pedal, opened his jacket and lifted his T-shirt, totally indifferent to the fact that they were traveling sixty miles per hour down the highway.

The Toyota swerved to the right, nearly down into a ditch before Connor got it back up on the pavement and under control.

The flesh on the left side of Terminator's chest was charred black, an area about the size of a package of cigarettes completely burned away, exposing his metal chassis.

With the Gerber blade, Terminator cut a long curving incision around the burned skin and muscle. There was no blood, and Terminator felt no pain. The skin was duraplast, a form of pliant plastic.

Connor had seen this kind of weirdness before, but he was still amazed. "What are you doing?"

"I am powered by two hydrogen fuel cells," Terminator said. He cut the flap of tissue free and casually tossed it out the door. "The primary cell has been damaged by the plasma cannon."

"Plasma cannon?" Connor said. The last time Skynet had sent a cyborg back to kill him, it hadn't been equipped with anything like that. "So this thing is worse than a T-1000?"

Terminator folded the knife blade and opened the prying tool that he used to release his chest plate. Next, he swung open a small panel that was just beneath the most severely burned area of flesh to expose complicated circuitry and a maze of mechanical works.

"That model was discontinued in 2029. The T-X is designed for extreme combat, driven by a plasma reactor and equipped with onboard weapons. It's a far more effective killing machine."

He opened the Gerber's pliers and got to work inside his chest.

"Okay, so she's like a tank with liquid metal skin," Connor said, and even he was having trouble believing what he was saying. "She can't be melted down?"

Terminator shook his head. It was an oddly human gesture, out of place with his chest open exposing the electromechanical innards. "The battle chassis is heavily armored, hardened to withstand external attack."

Connor shrugged. "You'll find a way to destroy her," he said, because it was his only hope for survival.

"Unlikely," Terminator replied, without looking up from his work. "I am an obsolete design. The T-X is faster, more powerful, more intelligent. Its arsenal includes nanotechnological transjectors."

"Meaning?" Connor asked.

Terminator glanced at Connor. "It can control other machines."

Connor nodded after a moment. He'd seen her handiwork with the police cars and ambulances. "Great," he muttered.

Terminator had gotten down to the pair of fuel cells in his chest. One of them smoked and sizzled. It was leaking something that was starting to react, like an acid, with his other circuitry, and a residual blue plasma energy still shifted and rippled like an aurora around the unit.

"My presence in this time has been anticipated. The T-X is designed to terminate other cybernetic organisms."

"So, she's an anti-terminator terminator," Connor said, working it out. He shook his head again. This was getting worse, much worse by the minute. "You've got to be shitting me," he mumbled.

"No," Terminator replied. "I am not shitting you."

He moved a pair of contacts, rerouting the last of his power circuits, then looked up for a moment as the circuitry displayed in his head-up unit confirmed that he had successfully isolated the damaged power cell.

Terminator handed the tool back to Connor, gingerly unplugged the power cell, and carefully removed it from his chest. It was about the size of a small book, and it looked battered, but not particularly dangerous.

With a snap of his wrist, Terminator threw the power

cell out into a sloping field of scrub brush and boulders. It arched one hundred feet into the morning sky, hanging at apogee for a long moment before it came down, a thousand feet off the highway.

When it hit the ground it exploded with a tremendous flash-bang. The shock wave hammered off the nearby foothills and slammed into the pet van, nearly shoving it off the road. Terminator had to help bring the Toyota back under control.

"When ruptured, the fuel cells become unstable," he said.

He pulled down his T-shirt and zippered his jacket to hide the surgery as Connor glanced back at the sizable mushroom cloud rising out of the field.

An hour later they were over the foothills and headed down toward the desert, the Toyota's gas gauge on empty, wisps of steam coming from under the hood.

A large gas station-truck stop-convenience store was nestled up against a low hump in the desert.

"We must stop here for fuel and coolant fluid," Terminator said. "Do you require supplies?"

"Something to eat, maybe some water, would be okay," Connor said. "Where are you taking us?"

Terminator ignored the question. He slowed down and pulled into the gas station just as the Toyota's engine began to buck and stall, finally out of gas. He coasted to a stop at one of the pumps, got out, and went into the store, leaving Connor to fill it up, check the oil, and get some water into the radiator.

No one was inside the station except for the cashier behind the counter. He was a teenager, wearing a striped cowboy shirt and a baseball cap. He could see the battered condition of the pet van, and the still obvious injuries to Terminator's face, though much of the skin had reformed, hiding the metal cranial case. It made him nervous.

Terminator took a moment to scan the contents of the store, spread down four aisles with rows of coolers along the back wall. He picked up a basket and walked up and down the aisles, methodically selecting various food items including beef jerky for protein, potato chips for carbohydrates, cookies, ice cream bars, and Twinkies for sugar, and bottled water for hydration.

The cashier was fiddling with a small television set behind the counter, but every channel he switched to displayed the same message: PLEASE STAND BY.

He had taped a hand-lettered sign in front of the cash register. NO CREDIT CARDS—COMPUTERS DOWN.

"Man, this is crazy," the kid said, switching to another channel that showed the same PLEASE STAND BY message. "It's been like this for hours. Every goddamned station."

Terminator stopped at a rack of sunglasses, studied the styles for a second, and then picked a pair of Sama wraparounds and put them on.

He turned and headed for the door.

The cashier looked up from the television set. "Hey, man, you gonna pay for that?"

Terminator ignored him.

"Hey," the cashier shouted.

Terminator pulled up short, turned to the kid, then stuck out the palm of his hand, just like the stripper had done to him in the desert roadhouse. "Talk to the hand."

The cashier shrank back, not sure what to do, and Terminator turned and walked out the door.

Connor was just finishing with the water in the radiator. He set the can aside and closed the hood.

Terminator unbent the lug wrench locking the pet van's back door with one hand and pulled it open.

Kate leaped out past him. "Help!" she screamed. "Help me!"

Terminator wrapped his free arm around her waist before she took two steps and pulled her back.

Kate suddenly attacked him like a madwoman, kneeing him in the groin with every ounce of her strength, chopping his windpipe, driving her thumbs under his sunglasses deep into the sockets of his eyes.

Terminator was not affected. His diagnostic circuits were clear of any serious damage indicators.

He gently pried her away and shoved her back into the pet van. He adjusted his sunglasses, which had been knocked askew, then placed the basket of groceries in back with her.

Connor, who had watched everything, spotted the cashier through the window. The kid was on the phone. Probably calling for help.

"I think we should go," he said.

Terminator nodded indifferently, and he went around

to the driver's side as Connor climbed in back with Kate and closed the door.

Kate was huddled again in the corner, her knees up to her chin. She braced herself as the pet van took off and swerved sharply back out onto the highway.

Connor didn't know how he felt about her now that he knew she would become an important part of the human resistance. But she sure could fight. He had to grin.

"You've got some good moves on you," he told her. A flash of something came to him. "I remember now. You were like an army brat or something, right?"

Kate didn't look at him. He pushed the basket of food over to her. "Ice cream?" he suggested.

She kicked the basket away, scattering the contents. Connor held up his hands and shrugged. "Okay," he said in an effort to be conciliatory.

"You're kidnapping me," she said after a few moments.

"Look, I—"

"God, you were always a delinquent," Kate said. It was as if a dam had broken inside her. The words came out in an angry rush. "And look at you now. Sitting there like the bad boy thing still works." She gave him an extremely critical once-over. "What are you, some kind of a gang member? A drug dealer?" She was disgusted. Her loathing dripped from her tongue and attitude like venom. "How do you live with yourself?" she asked.

Connor shook his head, another smile coming to his lips. How was he supposed to tell her the real story when he had trouble believing it himself?

Kate's nostrils flared. She thought he was laughing at her. "What?" she demanded.

Connor rapped on the divider window, and Terminator slid it open. "Tell her who I am," Connor said.

"John Connor is the leader of the worldwide resistance and the last best hope of mankind."

Kate shook her head again. It was painfully obvious that she thought they were raving lunatics, probably high on something. "Right," she said. "And him?" She nodded toward Terminator.

"He's a robot from the future. Living tissue over a metal skeleton. Sent back in time to—"

Kate sat back morosely. She was tired of the game. "Go to hell."

"He doesn't mean you any harm," Connor assured her, knowing how this must sound.

Kate held up her left hand, showing him her engagement diamond. "I have a fiancé. He's going to be looking for me."

Connor sat back too, suddenly morose. His mood matched hers. If Terminator was right about the abilities of the T-X, they didn't stand much of a chance.

Kate watched him. "I . . . What is it you *want*?"

Connor lowered his eyes. "I don't know," he answered. And it was the truth. He didn't know what he really wanted. He looked up after a beat. How to tell her? What words? "I guess . . . Imagine if you know you were going to do something important with your life. Something amazing. Maybe the most important thing anyone's ever done."

He had her attention. She looked at him in a slightly different light, though it was clear that she didn't understand what he was trying to say. But she was beginning to believe his sincerity.

"But there's a catch. Something terrible has to happen. You couldn't live with yourself if you didn't try to stop it. But if you do . . . The rest of your life is pointless."

"What's *that* supposed to mean?" Kate asked.

"I mean someone normal. Someone sane—" He wanted her to understand. "It's just that . . . The life you know, all the stuff you take for granted, it's not going to last."

She still wasn't getting it. Connor could see the skepticism and confusion in her pretty eyes. And there was something else. Something in the way she held herself. Something in the way that she was looking at him at that moment that seemed familiar. It was something she'd said to him earlier.

"Wait. Back at the clinic. Why did you say, 'Mike Kripke's basement'?"

Kate didn't answer.

Connor was suddenly remembering. "Kripke's house. That's where the kids used to make out." He was trying to bring it all back. "So you and me. Did we—?"

Kate looked away, more uncomfortable now than confused.

"Holy shit—we did!" Connor said. "We made out in Kripke's basement. I can't believe you remembered."

Still Kate held her silence, but a slight color had come to her neck.

"I guess I must've made quite an impression," Connor said.

Kate turned on him. "Gimme a break. I only remembered because the next day you were in the news."

Suddenly the impossibility of the coincidence dropped into place for Connor. He glanced through the mesh at Terminator, then back at Kate.

"You and I hooked up the day before I first met him? And then again now, twelve years later?"

"Right," Kate said sarcastically. "We were supposed to meet. Fate, right?" She shook her head. "Coincidence."

But it wasn't coincidence and Connor knew it. "Yeah," he said to appease her, nothing more. He glanced at the back of Terminator's head. "What *was* going on?"

The Valley

The bedroom was still dark because the shades were drawn. Kate's nightshirt lay on the floor where she'd tossed it a few hours ago, and her fiancé, Scott Peterson, was still asleep in the double bed.

T-X stood in the doorway, cataloguing the homey scene. Kate had not returned yet, but she would have to come back here sooner or later.

Either that or someone would come looking for her. She was the key to finding John Connor again. Her fiancé was expendable.

T-X moved silently across the room and sat down on

Kate's side of the bed. She picked a framed photo off the nightstand and studied it. It was Katherine Brewster at her graduation. Robert Brewster stood beside her. Smiling. The proud father.

Scott stirred on the bed. T-X put the photo back as Scott sat up. "Hon? You just get in?"

T-X swiveled her torso 180 degrees to face Scott, who stared at her with incomprehension. She reached over with one hand, almost gently caressing the man's face, before she lowered her hand, thrust it deep into his chest, and destroyed his heart before he could utter a sound.

He fell back in a bloody heap.

T-X went to the bathroom where she fastidiously washed the blood from her hand as the front doorbell rang.

She cocked her head, her sensors picking up electronic emissions from a plain sedan parked on the street. Police frequency emissions.

She glanced at Scott's body, then headed to the living room, her body thickening, her clothing melting away and changing so that by the time she opened the front door she had assumed the infiltration mode of Scott Peterson, including the boxer shorts and T-shirt he wore for bed.

Two men stood in the corridor; one a bald white man, the other a black man with short dark hair. They were dressed in cheap suits and ties.

They held out their gold shields. "Detective Martinez, LAPD," the one introduced himself. "We're looking for Katherine Brewster. Is she here?"

T-X, as Scott Peterson, shook his head.

The detective consulted his notebook. "You're her fiancé, Scott Peterson?"

T-X nodded.

"A few hours ago there was an incident at the veterinary hospital where she works. We're concerned something might have happened to her."

"Where is she?" T-X asked without inflection, as if the Scott character were in shock.

"Well, we got a report from a gas station attendant out toward Victorville about a possible kidnapping. Might be related."

T-X nodded his head. "I can help you find her."

The two detectives glanced at each other and nodded. "Sure. Any idea where she might have gone?"

Valley of Peace Cemetery

In the back of the pet van John Connor watched through the dividing window over Terminator's shoulder.

He and Kate had finally eaten something and had drunk some water, but she refused to say anything else to him. He almost hated to turn his back on her. She looked as if she were on the verge of going berserk again. There was no telling what she was capable of doing.

Connor hadn't been able to figure out where they were going, although he knew that the desert was off to the east and L.A. back the other way. But now they were in an area of grass and tree-covered rolling hills, the occasional long driveway up to a house in the distance, or a small horse ranch nestled against a steeper hill. Pleasant countryside. He figured that a lot of people escaping from the daily grind in Los Angeles came out here.

Terminator drove at a steady sixty miles per hour, on the straight stretches or on the curves, it didn't seem to matter to him.

They were off the main highway, on a blacktopped secondary road that suddenly came around a hill to a broad vista of trees, grassy slopes, and narrow roads that wound their way in and among headstones, classical statues, small family plots enclosed by low iron picket fences, and mausoleums of all sizes, styles, and ornateness.

No one seemed to be here this morning, except for a hearse and a Cadillac limousine parked at the base of a hill in the distance. At the top was a Gothic stone building that was an entrance to a crypt. But there didn't seem to be any people nearby. Nor were there any signs that caretakers were at work this early.

Without slowing down, Terminator made the sharp turn onto the entrance road, flashed past a sign that read VALLEY OF PEACE CEMETERY, and crashed straight through a tall iron gate, knocking it half off its hinges.

He drove directly across the cemetery, following the narrow roads, finally slowing down and coming to a halt near where the hearse and the limousine were parked.

The morning was cool and beautiful out here, the sun very bright in a crystal clear sky.

Terminator opened the rear door. Connor jumped out first, blinking in the brightness. He turned and offered his hand to Kate, but she batted it away and jumped down on her own.

"Come with me," Terminator said. He turned and strode up the hill to the crypt entrance that was flanked by tall stained-glass windows showing angels ascending to heaven. Connor almost expected to hear organ music playing softly.

The heavy bronze doors were locked, but Terminator

simply pulled them open as if they had been held in place by straw.

Inside, he led them down a flight of stairs into the crypt. Coffins were set behind marble slabs in tombs that were stacked five high. The morning light was diffused and colored by the windows, lending the place the solemn air it was supposed to have.

Connor suddenly had an uneasy feeling that he knew who was buried here, but he couldn't stop himself from seeing with his own eyes.

Terminator stopped in front of one of the tombs near the center of the crypt.

Connor pulled up short, hesitating, as he saw what was chiseled in the marble cover of the tomb. He'd never been here before. He didn't even know about this place.

He took a few steps closer, Kate just behind him. The inscription read SARAH CONNOR—1959–1997—NO FATE BUT WHAT WE MAKE.

Kate was obviously confused. Nothing that had happened to her this morning made any sense. She looked from the inscription on the tomb to Terminator and then to Connor.

"Your mother?" she asked.

"I never knew where she was buried," he said, his voice soft but filled with emotion. "I hit the road the day she died." He looked at Terminator. "Why did you bring me here?"

Terminator didn't answer. Without warning he slammed his fist through the marble slab, shattering it into a million pieces, sending chunks flying everywhere, dust rising from the pulverized stone.

Connor couldn't believe what was happening. He tried to muscle the cyborg aside, but it was like ramming his shoulder into a brick wall. "No! What are you doing?"

Terminator shoved him away, reached into the tomb, and pulled out the polished stainless-steel coffin with one hand as if it were a toy. He slammed it on the floor, popped the locking bolts out of their seats, and threw open the lid.

Connor was speechless. He didn't know exactly what he expected to see after all these years; his mother's skeleton, probably. But he wasn't expecting to find a steel coffin completely crammed with weapons and loads. A .30-caliber machine gun, several Russian-made AK-47 assault rifles, 9mm Glock pistols, a bandolier of H&W stun grenades that U.S. Special Forces used, a LAW antitank rocket, a 40mm Mk-19 grenade launcher with its loads, small bricks of C-4 plastic explosive, and a lot of other weapons, all of which Connor knew how to use.

"Sarah Connor was cremated in Mexico," Terminator explained. "Her friends scattered her ashes in the sea. They stored these weapons in accordance with her will."

Connor's eyes were drawn away from the weapons to a larger piece of the marble tomb on which the name CONNOR was legible. So many years wasted. So many lives lost. So much damage and heartache.

Now this.

"What happened to her?" Kate asked at Connor's shoulder.

"Leukemia."

"I'm sorry," she said, staring at the weapons.

Terminator was going through them, checking to see what had been left behind, in what condition everything was, and discarding some of the things.

"We were living down in Baja when she was diagnosed," Connor said, not looking up. He was still in his own thoughts. Still back in Mexico with his mother. "They gave her only six months, but she fought for three years." He lowered his eyes. "Long enough to make sure."

"Make sure?" Kate prompted.

"That the world didn't end," he said. His life for the past twelve years had been surreal. But these past four hours had been the worst. " 'Every day after this one is a gift,' she told me. 'We made it, we're free.' But I never really believed it." He glanced at the weapons. "I guess she didn't either."

He and Terminator looked at each other.

"You know, you were the closest thing I ever had to a father," Connor told him. He shook his head. "How pathetic is that?"

Kate suddenly lunged between them, snatched a Glock 17 pistol from the coffin, and skipped back a couple of steps as she fumbled for the twin triggers. Her father had taught her something about guns too.

Terminator stepped to the left, blocking her exit.

She pointed the pistol at his face. "Out of my way!" The gun trembled in her grip.

"My mission is to protect you," Terminator told her

evenly. He took a step toward her and she backed up, keeping the gun trained on him.

"That's enough," she warned. She took another step back and was at the wall. There was nowhere to go. She tightened her grip on the gun and steadied her aim. "Move, or I'll do it. I swear I will. I'll shoot you!"

Connor hadn't moved. "Go ahead," he told her. "See what happens."

Kate was distracted by what Connor was suggesting. She glanced at him to make sure that he wasn't laughing at her again.

Terminator snatched the weapon out of Kate's hand. Her finger jerked the triggers back, past the safety guard, and the weapon fired point-blank into his face.

He flinched, and Kate stepped aside in horror, stifling a scream, not believing what she had just done.

Terminator rolled something around in his mouth, turned his head, and spat out the deformed bullet, a drop of artificial blood on his lips.

"Don't do that," he said mildly.

Kate was beside herself. She didn't know what to do. Where to turn. What to say. "Oh, my God," she muttered. "Oh, my God."

Something metallic banged against the entry corridor wall and clattered down the stairs with a tremendous racket, belching dense white smoke.

It was tear gas. Connor jumped back from the canister as the sharply pungent smoke filled his nostrils and burned his eyes like acid. He had been taught as a kid to breathe shallowly when you found yourself in this kind of situation. But Kate wouldn't know that.

"This is the police," a powerfully amplified voice came from outside the crypt. "We have the building surrounded. Release your hostage."

Connor reached for Kate, but she spun on her heel, managed to skip past Terminator, and was gone up the stairs in a flash.

He tried to go after her, but Terminator kicked the tear gas canister aside and hauled Connor back to a relatively smoke-free niche behind a couple of marble statues of angels.

"Just leave me here," Connor protested. His eyes were red and filled with tears. His vision was blurry at best. "You're wasting your time. I'm not the one you want."

"Incorrect," Terminator replied firmly. "John Connor leads the resistance to victory."

"How?" Connor shouted. "Why? Why me?"

"You are John Connor," Terminator said without inflection, as if Connor had just questioned a fundamental law of the universe.

But Connor shook his head. "Christ, my mom fed me that bullshit from the cradle. But look at me. I'm no leader. I never was. I'm never gonna be."

Terminator grabbed Connor by the throat and lifted him bodily off the floor so that they were eye to eye.

Connor struggled desperately to get free. "What are you—Let go—"

Terminator squeezed harder, as if he were going to

choke the life out of the human. "You are right," he said. "You are not the one I want. I am wasting my time."

Connor's eyes went wide with rage. The injustice of what was happening to him now was beyond bearing. After all he had gone through. After his mother. After everything. The struggle. All the bullshit for twelve years.

Not this way. He wasn't going to die here and now. Not this way. He slammed his hands into the sides of Terminator's skull, kicking, thrashing wildly, fighting for his life with a rage that threatened to blot out every last sane thought in his head.

"Fuck you!" Connor screamed raggedly. "You fucking machine!"

Terminator nodded. "Better," he said. He tossed Connor aside.

Connor picked himself up and rubbed his throat as he tried to catch his breath. He had been close to fuzzing out. "Why did you do that?" he croaked.

But Terminator showed little or no reaction.

"You were dicking with me?" Connor demanded.

"Anger is more useful than despair."

"What?"

"Basic psychology is among my subroutines," Terminator said as if he were discussing the weather. He pulled the modified Stoner 63A .30-caliber machine gun out of the coffin, then grabbed a belt of ammunition and efficiently loaded the weapon, pulled the slide back and released the safety.

Connor suddenly remembered what Terminator was capable of doing. "Jesus, don't kill them."

"My reprogramming will not allow it. I am incapable of taking human life."

Connor grinned wryly, still rubbing his bruised neck. "Good to know."

Near Victorville

They had left the BP station a few minutes ago. The black detective was driving the plain blue Chevy sedan, while his partner, Detective Martinez, spoke to someone by cell phone. Something was haywire with all the police frequencies, but so far cell phones didn't seem to be affected.

T-X, as Scott Peterson, dressed now in a light sweater and slacks, sat in the backseat listening. There was trouble not too far away from here. The San Bernadino County Sheriff's office and State Police had been called in, along with an LAPD SWAT team.

"Perps are still holed up?" Detective Martinez said. He nodded. "Gotcha." He broke the connection and turned to T-X. "Good news, your girlfriend's okay."

"Where is she?" T-X asked.

Martinez glanced forward. "Valley of Peace Cemetery. But they're going to bring her downtown—"

T-X drove its left hand through the back of the front seat, its fist emerging from the black detective's chest, the fingers grabbing the steering wheel in a spray of blood, shattered bone, and torn tissue.

Martinez reared back, not able to grasp what he was witnessing except that it was bad. Worse than he'd ever seen.

"Oh, Jesus, God——" he blurted.

He grabbed for his piece beneath his jacket, but T-X smashed the man's head into the passenger side window with its free hand, breaking out the glass and shattering the detective's skull.

T-X drilled into the Chevy's dash panel and connected with the automobile's computers. The cemetery was highlighted on a map in its head-up display.

Its arm still through the detective's chest, T-X hauled the car into an accelerating U-turn and headed off.

Valley of Peace Cemetery

The LAPD SWAT team leader hustled Kate down the hill to one of the waiting ambulances, where he turned her over to a paramedic whose name tag read STEWART.

Police radio units, the SWAT team van, and fire rescue units were parked along the base of the hill thirty yards from where the hearse and Cadillac limousine were parked. No one had found the drivers of the two vehicles. They had probably taken off the moment the trouble started.

Officers, some of them dressed in dark jump suits with visored riot helmets and Kevlar vests, armed with various weapons including the Colt Commando assault rifle and the 9mm Heckler & Koch MP5 room broom, were fanned out behind headstones, statues, and one of the large mausoleums near the crypt.

Other cops were positioned behind their squad cars, their sidearms drawn. Still others held shotguns at the ready.

Dense clouds of tear gas poured from the entrance to the crypt as shell after shell was fired through the open doorway.

Kate shivered, and the paramedic put a blanket around her shoulders.

A heavyset man, with thinning white hair and a smarmy look on his round face, came over. He had a manner that Kate supposed was meant to be comforting.

"You're safe now," he told her.

She couldn't determine if he was for real or not. But then he hadn't seen that thing that had kidnapped her.

He dropped the cigarette he'd been smoking and ground it out. "Kate, my name is Dr. Silberman. I'm a post-trauma counselor for the Los Angeles County Sheriff's Department." He smiled pleasantly, trying to reassure her that everything would be okay. "How are you feeling?"

"He's not human," Kate said softly. "He's really not human—"

An understanding look came into Silberman's eyes. He sat down next to her in the back of the ambulance. "I know what it's like to be in a hostage situation. I've been there myself." He looked away and stared into the distance. He *had* been there. He *knew*. "The fear, the adrenaline. You find yourself imagining things. Impossible things. It can take years to get over it."

Six SWAT cops wearing gas masks made a dash for the entrance to the crypt, leapfrogging by twos so that they could provide covering fire for each other if need be.

Kate shrank back, but Silberman patted her hand. "It'll be fine, you'll see."

One of the stained-glass windows burst outward in a spray of colored glass shards. Terminator stepped through the opening. The machine gun was cradled in his right arm, and with his left he balanced the stainless-steel coffin on his shoulder. Dense smoke swirled around him.

The SWAT chief waiting farther down the hill raised his megaphone. "Drop your weapon." His sharply amplified voice rolled across the cemetery. "And the coffin!"

Terminator headed down the hill away from the crypt toward the pet van without breaking stride, looking neither left nor right.

Kate's heart hammered out of her chest. Dr. Silberman jumped to his feet.

The SWAT team at the entrance to the crypt swung around and opened fire. Bullets slammed into Terminator's back, ricocheted off the coffin with angry whines, and tumbled away at oblique angles.

They crab-walked behind him down the hill, laying down a continuous line of intense fire. Some of the bullets struck the pet van, opening the gas tank, and it caught fire with a dull thump.

Terminator paused momentarily, then turned and took a couple of steps toward the hearse parked about twenty yards away. He was still taking heavy fire to his torso, his legs, and to the back of his head.

He stopped again, raised the Stoner machine gun, and began spraying the cemetery in a long, looping arc; the large caliber bullets shattered headstones, cut down small trees and statues, and destroyed several police cars.

His targeting computer, which showed up as a reticle in his head-up display, overlaid with the heat signatures of humans, was meticulous in avoiding nonmechanical targets.

The police officers and SWAT team crew dove for cover.

Silberman's face turned ghostly white. He stammered something incomprehensible.

Kate got to her feet, the blanket falling off, and she backed away from the ambulance. "They can't stop him," she babbled. "We have to get out of here—"

She turned, but Silberman was already gone, running as fast as his legs could carry him from the battle zone.

"Oh, God," Kate cried, and she started after him.

Terminator reached the hearse during a momentary lull in the return fire. He tore open the rear door, shoved the coffin inside, and slammed the door shut.

The police units opened fire again as he moved around to the driver's side, got in behind the wheel, yanked the ignition set out of the steering column, and hot-wired the engine.

Bullets had retorn the flesh from Terminator's neck and head, exposing bits of his metallic cranial case, but doing nothing other than superficial damage to his main systems.

The hearse was beginning to take fire, some of the windows blowing out, bullets slapping against the sheet metal like hammer taps in a tinsmith's shop.

The lid of the coffin opened, and Connor, who'd been jammed inside with the weapons, rolled out, keeping below the level of the windows.

"Get us out of here!" he shouted.

The engine caught. "We must reacquire Katherine Brewster," Terminator said. He swiveled his head and did a quick scan of the cemetery with his sensors.

"Why?" Connor demanded. "What makes her so goddamn important?"

"Through her you make contact with the remnants of the U.S. military and learn to fight Skynet, forming the core of the resistance," Terminator said.

They were taking a lot of heavy fire, but Terminator acquired two moving targets. One of them was a 96.55534 percent probable match to Katherine Brewster. He slammed the hearse into low and peeled out.

"Later, your children become important when—" Terminator continued as if nothing else were happening.

"Whoa," Connor stopped him. "What?"

"She is your wife," Terminator said, matter-of-factly.

Silberman had disappeared, and the shooting was still going on behind her. Kate had no one to turn to. She didn't think the cops stood a chance against that—thing. Not after what she'd seen it do.

A dark blue Chevy sedan came roaring up the road and through the broken gate into the cemetery. Someone was slumped in the front seat.

Kate pulled up short as the car screeched to a halt fifty feet away. The back door popped open and Scott jumped out.

Instant relief poured over her like ice water on a blistering hot day. She couldn't believe it. Scott. Here.

"Scott," she cried, starting for him. "Thank God!"

T-X moved toward Kate, morphing, as he seemed to glide over the grass, back into the persona of Nancy Nebel in the rust-colored Gucci leather suit.

Her right arm was changing into the plasma weapon, and Kate stopped in midstride.

This was the same monster from the pet clinic. The one who had killed Betsy. The one who had nearly killed them all.

"No—" Kate moaned, stepping back. Was there no end to this insanity?

T-X raised her plasma weapon, the blue glow surrounding her arm as the unit came to a full charge.

Valley of Peace Cemetery

"Give me an RPG," Terminator ordered.

"You said you can't kill anybody," Connor argued.

"John. The RPG. Now."

Connor had spotted the heavier Russian-made RPG-7 Rocket Propelled Grenade Launchers in the coffin. He'd practiced with them in Baja a couple of years before his mother had died. One of her biker friends had come up from Honduras or someplace like that with a bunch of shit.

He dug one of the weapons out of the coffin, loaded the 85mm shell, and slapped it into Terminator's outstretched right hand.

The rocket, which carried a five-pound HEAT warhead, could penetrate a foot of armored steel plate. The Russians had built them to bust tanks. Terrorists used them to stop cops.

Connor was trying to figure out what Terminator wanted to shoot at. He suddenly spotted Kate standing alone, her hand up, as if she were trying to ward off an attack.

Then he saw the T-X, her right arm engulfed in a blue glow, pointing the plasma cannon directly at Kate.

"It's Kate," he shouted.

Driving with his left hand, Terminator rested the tube of the RPG on the windowsill across his chest. He uncaged the firing circuit and without hesitation pulled the trigger.

The shell was ejected from the tube, and about fifteen feet out its rocket motor ignited, propelling it almost instantly the last few meters to the T-X's right arm just as the plasma cannon was firing.

A sharp, bright explosion engulfed the T-X's weapon arm, staggering her backward a few feet. A split second later the misfiring cannon erupted in a huge blue flash-bang that hurled the cyborg off her feet, sending her flying twenty meters onto her back.

Terminator veered the hearse sharply to the right, just missing a row of headstones, and slid to a stop next to an openmouthed Kate, who seemed to be rooted to the ground where she stood.

Connor reached over and opened the passenger door. "Get in," he shouted to her.

She didn't move. The cops were charging toward them, guns drawn, but the firing had stopped for the moment. But only for the moment.

"Do you want to live?" Connor shouted. "Come on!"

Kate looked over to where the T-X had already gotten to her feet. The cyborg's weapon was a mangled ruin, but she ripped off the tip of the cannon and the artificial skin began to form over the machinery. She was damaged but not out of commission.

T-X looked up, and started for the hearse.

Move or die, the thought was like a high-power bolt of electricity to Kate's brain. She jumped into the hearse and pulled the door shut.

Terminator slammed the gas pedal to the floor and the hearse shot across the cemetery, spewing grass and dirt from its back wheels.

He glanced in the rearview mirror as the T-X picked up speed, crashing through gravestones as if they were not there.

But she was not gaining on the hearse. The dispersal of the plasma energy had apparently caused an overload in her power circuits. But that reduced capacity would not last for long. Terminator had been programmed with what few specs the resistance had managed to gather. Among them was the T-X model's ability to recharge its own power cells. The tiny fusion generator in its chest cavity took a finite amount of time to replace such a large loss of power, but the recharge time was very short.

Measured not in minutes, but in seconds.

Terminator hauled the hearse around a mausoleum, bumped up onto the driveway, and shot through the gate back to the blacsktopped highway.

The T-X was no longer visible in the rearview mirror.

"What the hell was that thing?" Kate demanded. She was all out of breath. "Why is it after me? What did I do?"

"It's what you're going to do," Connor said from the back. He pulled out another RPG rocket in case the T-X caught up with them. "You're important in the future. We both are."

Terminator headed to the highway that led away from L.A. and back out onto the desert.

There was almost no traffic, only an occasional farmer in his pickup or delivery truck, and a tractor pulling a flat wagon on car tires loaded with hay.

There would almost certainly be police units, but for the moment the only thing that Terminator's sensors were picking up was a helicopter. Judging by its attempt at radio communications it was probably a police chopper outbound from Los Angeles.

Kate looked nervously from Terminator to Connor, fear and uncertainty in her eyes. "It was Scott," she said. "How could it be Scott?"

"Your fiancé?" Connor asked.

Kate nodded, Unable to speak.

"The T-X is polymimetic, able to take the form of anything it touches," Terminator told her with no hint of emotion. "Your fiancé is dead."

Kate's complexion paled. She looked like a ghost.

Connor had to wince at Terminator's lack of tact, but he kept his eyes on the road behind them. The T-X would not stop coming after them. Not until her entire chassis was destroyed.

If such a thing were possible.

"Looks like we lost her," he said without much conviction. It was mostly wishful thinking on his part.

The road swept around the base of a steep, boulder-strewn, wooded hill. The embankment loomed close to the highway.

The T-X suddenly emerged from the woods at the top of the hill at a dead run and leaped out into space, landing with a tremendous bang on top of the hearse.

The roof was crushed inward almost to the level of the coffin by the impact of the T-X's 150-kilo mass. The back windows shattered into thousands of pieces, and the windshield starred but held in place.

Connor had just pulled an AK-47 assault rifle and a thirty-round box magazine out of the coffin. He barely managed to roll left and flatten himself on the floor before he was trapped by the collapsing roof.

The hearse swerved sharply left, nearly off the road and down into a ditch before Terminator was able to bring it under control.

Kate screamed in absolute terror, crouching as low as she could get in the front seat.

A high-pitched angry whine came from above the hearse, and suddenly the lower half of a circular saw cut through the roof in a shower of sparks.

Terminator hauled the hearse to the right, laying rubber on the highway as he slammed on the brakes.

He immediately jammed the gas pedal to the floor and swerved sharply left in an effort to dislodge the T-X from the roof.

But it did not work.

The T-X's left arm had morphed into a high-speed metal cutting saw that was opening a U-shaped flap in the roof as easily as a razor blade through tissue paper.

"Do something!" Kate screeched in desperation.

Terminator ignored her. A map of the rural area was overlaid in his head-up display with a thermal imaging picture. The road they were on intersected with the highway in three hundred meters. Barreling down the highway from the west was the heat signature of what Terminator identified as an eighteen-wheeler.

His processors did the math, and he reduced his speed slightly to 71.3 miles per hour, which gave him the solution.

The saw retracted from the roof and the long, rectangular flap peeled open like the lid on a sardine can.

No longer hemmed in by the collapsed roof, Connor swung the AK-47 to bear on the T-X as he pulled the cocking slide back and flicked the safety catch forward.

He pulled the trigger, firing the 7.62mm rounds directly into her face, emptying the magazine in three seconds flat.

The T-X recoiled after each shot, but then came back to the opening and reached down to grab Connor, who scrambled a few inches forward just out of her grasp.

A semi's air horn suddenly blared right on top of them.

Terminator shoved Kate farther down in the seat as he hunched over, steering the hearse beneath the trailer just behind the turnbuckle with a last-moment burst of speed.

The roof and the T-X suddenly disappeared as the bottom of the semi trailer sheared off the top of the hearse with a shriek of tearing, twisting metal, breaking plastic, and shattering glass.

Connor got a split-instant glimpse of the semi's rear wheels less than one foot from the side of the hearse when they were on the other side and clear on the empty highway.

A tremendous wind roared through the now open hearse. Connor sat up cautiously as they rounded a curve, the semi sliding sideways across the highway behind them.

Kate sat up too. Tentatively, as if she couldn't believe that they had come through the crash alive.

Terminator was impassive. They had merely completed another phase of his assignment.

"We need a new vehicle," he said to no one in particular.

Kate looked at Connor and he couldn't help but laugh with relief. She laughed too. This was insane. All of it. His entire life. This morning. This moment.

T-X sat up. She had landed at the side of the road fifty meters from the jackknifed semi.

Her diagnostic circuits registered some damage to her infiltration overlay, but only superficial damage to her battle chassis.

The most severe damage had been done to her plasma cannon by the small missile's explosive warhead that had made a perfectly timed hit.

Her flesh retracted from the mangled discharge head

of the cannon. She studied the damage for a few milliseconds, her diagnostic-repair processor immediately devising a solution.

With her free hand she artfully twisted and bent the various plasma magnetic containment conduits into a new, much smaller, cruder transmission head.

Only a fraction of her available power could be transmitted with the new arrangement, but the repaired weapon would still be formidable.

The trucker jumped down from his rig and took a few steps up the road toward T-X. He was dazed, and still uncertain of what had happened.

T-X glanced at him. He was typical of humans of his socio-economic class in this era: round shoulders, potbelly, wearing a red baseball cap, yellow checked shirt, and dark trousers and work boots. Probably not well educated.

The trailer bore the advertising legend for something called XENADRINE EFX, with the advice, EXPERIENCE THE POWER.

Ignoring him, T-X raised her jury-rigged weapon and fired a short plasma burst at the side of the hill. Grass and bushes went up in flames and a small area of gravel and rocks was instantly reduced to slag.

Out of the corner of her optical sensors she saw the truck driver turn and run away as fast as his bandy legs could take him.

She would not kill him. He was meaningless.

Her electronic emissions detectors picked up the transmissions from what she determined to be an LAPD helicopter, flying at one hundred meters above the terrain, two kilometers away.

She adjusted her internal communications circuitry and made contact with the helicopter. "Nancy-one-zero-zero-niner, L.A. base," she radioed. "Copy?"

Angeles National Forest

Beneath the protection of a canopy of trees Connor stared at the empty, mostly cloudless sky.

There had been police activity all morning and into the afternoon. But it was coming up on two-thirty and he hadn't seen a spotter plane or helicopter in at least forty-five minutes.

Kate was still in a state of semishock. Other than drinking from the cool mountain stream, she hadn't spoken or moved to try to escape. Nothing.

The T-X was still out there, coming after them. If being crushed beneath a crane and fire truck hadn't destroyed her, then being struck by a semi truck had probably not even dented her armor.

Terminator had done something to the hearse's engine and he slammed the hood as Connor came over.

"It's been clear for almost an hour."

Terminator didn't bother looking up at the sky. "I am unable to fix this vehicle."

"Will it run?" Conner asked.

"Yes. But not long."

"Then let's find something else and get as far away as we can," Connor said.

They got back into the hearse and headed farther up into the mountains where within a couple of miles they passed twenty or twenty-five trout fishermen working the stream that was just off the road there. A registration table was set up under a bright red canopy. The sign flapping in the light breeze read FIFTH ANNUAL ANGELES FOREST TROUT FEST.

No one noticed the heavily damaged hearse as it passed, and minutes later they came across an RV campground filled with campers, but devoid of people. The RVs belonged to the fishermen in the trout contest downstream.

Terminator pulled alongside a midsized Winnebago that appeared to be in good condition, and shut off the hearse's engine. The motor bucked and dieseled for a few seconds and then died.

He got out, went over to the Winnebago, and yanked open its locked door.

Connor jumped out of the hearse. "Come on," he said to Kate. "We have to keep moving."

Terminator came back, scooped up an armful of weapons, and took them to the RV. Connor grabbed the AK-47 and a bag of magazines and brought them over to the Winnebago.

"He was killed because of me," Kate said from the passenger seat. She made no move to get out.

Connor gathered four canvas satchels of C-4 explosive and acid fuses. He stopped and looked at her. He could feel her pain. He knew what it was like to lose someone who was very close.

He shoved a 9mm Beretta pistol into his belt, first making sure that its magazine was loaded and the safety catch was engaged.

"I know it won't help, but sometimes things happen that we just can't change." He shook his head. He didn't know what to say to her. He didn't have words to make a difference. "It's not your fault."

Kate looked at him without moving, without saying a word.

Connor took the plastic explosives over to the RV and placed them inside. Terminator was there.

"You're sure about this?" Connor asked him, keeping his voice low enough so that Kate couldn't hear him. "About her and me, I mean."

"I do not experience uncertainty," Terminator replied.

Connor laughed. "Must be nice to be you."

Terminator studied him for a moment. "Your confusion is not rational. She is a healthy female of breeding age."

"I think there's more to it than that," Connor said, feeling a little warmth at the base of his neck.

"My database does not encompass the dynamics of human pair bonding," Terminator said. He went back to the hearse for more weapons. Connor followed him.

"This Terminatrix, how many others does she have on her hit list?"

"Twenty-two," Terminator replied, gathering the belted ammunition for the machine gun. "Anderson, Elizabeth.

Anderson, William. Barrera, José. Brewster, Robert—"

Kate sat bolt upright, her eyes wide. "My father?" she demanded.

Terminator turned his optical sensors to her, noting her pupil dilation, the tightening at the corners of her mouth, and her increased heart and respiration rates. But there was no need to lie by omission at this time. "Having failed to acquire its primary target, the T-X will resume its default program."

Kate leaped out of the hearse. It looked as if she was getting ready to spring at Terminator or at Connor. She just hadn't made up her mind. "She's going to kill my father too?"

"There is a high probability."

"No," Kate shrieked. "No!"

This was something new, and it wasn't making sense to Connor. "Who is he? What does he do?"

"He's in the Air Force," Kate snapped. "Weapons design. Secret stuff." She pushed her hair off her forehead. "I don't know exactly—"

Terminator started back to the Winnebago with another load of weapons. He stopped. "General Robert Brewster is program director at CRS—Cyber Research Systems—Autonomous Weapons Division."

Suddenly it began to make sense to Connor. "Autonomous Weapons—Skynet. You're talking about Skynet, aren't you?"

"Skynet is one of the digital defense systems developed under Brewster's supervision."

"Oh, God," Connor said. Everything was crystal clear

now. Chillingly clear. "It all makes sense now." He shook his head in amazement. "If you hadn't come back when I was a kid, if everything hadn't changed, she and I—" He glanced at Kate. "She and I, we would've gotten together then. I would have met her father a long time ago, and—" There was even more. It was unrolling like a gigantic map in his mind's eye. "Do you see? This was *always* supposed to happen."

Kate shook her head in confusion. It was clear she had no idea what he was talking about. "I don't understand."

"Your father, this is all about your father," Connor told her excitedly. "He's the key! He always was—not Cyberdyne. Don't you see? We couldn't stop them from creating the technology. That part was inevitable, but we can stop it from being used. Your father's the one who can shut Skynet down. He's the only one who ever could." His jaw tightened. He turned to Terminator. We have to get to him before the T-X does."

"Negative," Terminator said. "I cannot jeopardize my mission." He turned and went back to the Winnebago with his load of weapons.

"This *is* your mission!" Connor shouted after him. "To save people."

Terminator turned. "My mission is to ensure the survival of John Connor and Katherine Brewster."

"I'm giving you an order," Connor said with a sharp edge in his voice.

"I am not programmed to follow your orders," Terminator replied indifferently. He put the weapons into the

RV. "After the nuclear war you will both lead."

"Nuclear war?" Kate shouted. This was way over the top for her, even after everything else she had been put through this day.

"There doesn't have to be a war," Connor insisted.

Terminator went back to the hearse for another load. Connor grabbed his arm to pull him back, but it was like trying to stop a moving locomotive.

"We can stop it," Connor told him.

"There is insufficient time. The first launch sequences will be initiated at 6:18 P.M."

Connor was caught flat-footed. "Today?" he blurted.

"Affirmative," Terminator said.

Connor was more deeply shocked than he'd ever been in his life; even more unsure of what he was supposed to do than he had been the first time Terminator had come for him and his mother.

"John, what is he saying?" Kate asked.

"Judgment Day," he told her, but he didn't take his eyes off Terminator. "The end of the world. It's today. Three hours from now."

"Two hours and fifty-three minutes," Terminator said precisely. "We must continue south into Mexico to escape the primary blast zones."

"We have to get to her dad."

"The Mojave area sustains significant nuclear fallout. You will not survive."

"You mean we just run and hide in a hole somewhere while the bombs fall?"

Terminator looked Connor in the eye. "It is your destiny." He said it as if there were no other possibility.

But there were other possibilities. Connor looked away toward the distant desert. If he and Kate were supposed to become the leaders of the human resistance in some future time, why couldn't they begin right now? Here and now by doing something—one thing—to try to stop Judgment Day. Nothing was inevitable. His mother had drummed into his head fate was what we made it.

He glanced at Kate, then back at Terminator, and made his decision.

He pulled the pistol from his belt, switched off the safety, and pressed the muzzle to his own temple.

"Fuck my destiny," he said with determination.

Terminator moved toward him, but Connor held up a warning finger, and he stopped.

"John . . . ?" Kate asked uncertainly.

"You cannot self-terminate," Terminator said.

"No, *you* can't," Connor told him. "I can do whatever the hell I want. I'm a human being, not a goddamn robot."

"Cybernetic organism," Terminator automatically corrected.

"Whatever," Connor said. He girded himself. "Either we go to her father, get him to shut down Skynet, and stop this shit from ever happening, or so much for the great John Connor."

He pressed the muzzle of the gun a little harder against his temple. He would do it if he had to.

"Your future, my destiny—" Connor's jaw tightened

in anger. "I don't want any part of it. I never did."

Terminator's sensors did a complete body scan of Connor. "Based on your pupil dilation, skin temperature, and motor functions, I calculate an eighty-three percent probability that you will not pull the trigger."

Kate took a step toward Terminator. "Please, do what he says." She glanced at Connor, then back. "You have to save my father."

Terminator watched the subtle interplay between Kate and John. He nodded, the gesture very human. He came to a decision in the same way most humans came to decisions, by weighing all the options and possible outcomes.

"We can reach CRS in approximately one hour, depending on traffic conditions."

He turned without another word or gesture, placed the last of the weapons and loads into the Winnebago, and then got behind the wheel, ripped the ignition set out of the steering column, and started the engine.

For a long time Connor stood very still, the pistol still held to his head. He had won. But at what cost?

He could hear the rippling water of the trout stream as it splashed over the rocks. He could hear the light breeze rustling the leaves. He could smell grass and sweet pine and perhaps even the dry, sandalwood odors of the distant desert.

Slowly he lowered the pistol. Kate stared at him, an unreadable expression in her eyes. He smiled at her.

They had gotten through another crisis.

There were more to come.

Cyber Research Systems
Edwards Air Force Base

Three-star General Robert Brewster paused in the doorway to the expansive CRS presentation lounge a few minutes after four. He was a compact man with short dark hair and an air of resigned authority. These had been a tough few days.

A dozen high-ranking civilians and Air Force officers with whom Brewster had worked over the past four years were seated in front of the big video screen watching the start of the new CRS disk.

The slick promotional piece, complete with multiplane graphics, computer-aided animation, music, and sound effects had cost the corporation nearly two million dollars, and that for only fifteen minutes of what his wife would have called techno babble.

But the promo disk wasn't meant for the Saturday matinees. It was targeted at key members of the Pentagon, many of them still skeptical, as well as a large segment of the Congress who thought the entire Skynet project was not only astronomically expensive, but exceedingly dangerous.

"Turning over our entire defense network to a goddamn computer is nothing but nuts," New York Representative Howard F. Stevenson argued. He was the ranking member on so many House oversight committees that the media called him Mr. Watchdog.

The disk was for Stevenson, if for no one else. Convince him, and everyone else would fall into line.

The CRS symbol, interlocked branches within a six-sided figure, came up on the screen with the words CYBER RESEARCH SYSTEMS.

The narrator, who was actually a tech sergeant from Andrews Air Force Base, spoke over the logo.

"Cyber Research Systems, America's first line of defense—creators of the weapons technology of tomorrow—invites you to preview the most exciting ordnance of the twenty-first century."

Music swelled from speakers around the room as the video ran through the opening montage of weapons and weapons systems: high-tech hydraulics, highly reflective metal surfaces, sculpted into compound curves, plastics, electronic circuitry, advanced electromechanical devices, the uses of which could only be guessed at, and finally the barrels of a deadly looking chaingun.

"No ordinary think tank, our mission here at CRS—to make human warfare a thing of the past—is just a funding cycle away."

General Brewster squared his shoulders and marched into the room. Yesterday and last night had been disasters, with outages throughout the system, from Alaska to Guam, and from Andrews outside Washington, D.C., to Ramstein outside Kaiserslautern, Germany, and even right here at Edwards.

None of them had gotten much sleep, and so far, today had been a repeat performance of putting out fires as fast as they popped up.

Now it was his task to begin selling a system he was no longer as sure of as he had been two days ago.

"Sorry I'm late, gentlemen," he said.

A young CRS executive operating the video system hit pause as Thomas S. Shelby, CRS's chief financial officer, looked up.

"We just got started, Bob. Take a seat," Shelby said.

Brewster slipped in next to the CRS money man.

"Once you all sign off, I'll send the promos to the Joint Chiefs and Armed Services Committee," Shelby's young assistant said. His name was Sherwood Olson. He was a Harvard MBA. He clicked the remote and the video came on.

"Say hello to the soldier of tomorrow," the narrator said.

The screen widened on a sleek, menacing robot, armed with an array of sensors in its small head structure, with heavy, articulated arms that ended in deadly looking chainguns. The machine moved nimbly on a pair of wide treads, and it was very tall, nearly eight feet.

"The T-1 battlefield robot. A fully autonomous ground offensive system."

It would have to be explained to the Washington

crowd that T-1 was deadly, but it was nothing more than a first generation. The T-1-7s were more sophisticated. But there were even better projects on the near horizon. Much better.

The narrator continued. "And in the air, the H-K aerial weapons system—or, as we like to call it, the Hunter-Killer."

An H-K drone hovered in midair, It looked like a futuristic, rotorless helicopter, armed with a variety of weapons systems, but with no pilot.

Like the T-1s, the Hunter-Killers were autonomous battlefield systems. They could think and fight for themselves.

The H-K fired a missile that homed in on a target tank in the distance, completely obliterating it.

"This isn't science fiction," the narrator assured his audience. "It's reality, thanks to our top-secret innovation—Skynet—the revolutionary, artificially intelligent battlefield management network."

The video displayed a computer screen that showed the Skynet worldwide network of satellites.

"From strategic weapons to the individual soldier in the field, Skynet is able to control it all."

A model of the neural net computer chip that Cyberdyne's Miles Bennet Dyson had used as the basis for the first models of Skynet came up on the screen. It looked otherworldly. From another time or place. From what could have been an alien, nonhuman mind. Brewster thought that Dyson had been anything but an ordinary man.

Without Dyson leading the way before his tragic death, there would have been no Cyber Research Systems, and certainly no Skynet.

On the screen, Boris Kuznetskov, one of the best chess players in the world, moved his white knight into a position threatening the black queen and king.

He played against a robotic arm of gleaming copper-gold metal, with finely articulated fingers. The Russian's board position appeared to be unbeatable.

"Not only can Skynet outthink the most inspired human adversary, but it designs the weapons it needs to meet its war-fighting plans.

"It is the definition of thinking outside the box."

The robotic arm moved a rook from a middle rank. Suddenly the outcome of the chess match wasn't so clear. The Russian was rattled.

"During this match alone, Skynet invented twenty-six thousand one hundred twenty-three new variations of chess, and over six million new moves."

It was clear that the Russian was defeated and he knew it.

"Meanwhile, human generals are still playing a four-thousand-year-old game," the narrator said.

Kuznetskov flipped over the chessboard in exasperation, looked bleakly at the robot arm, and then stalked off camera.

"Great leaders are not born," the narrator continued. "They're made. Right here. With technology developed at CRS."

Typical of multinational corporations, Brewster

thought. If something is said loud enough, often enough, and with absolute conviction, it will be believed.

"Actually the patents were obtained from a private vendor. Cyberdyne," he said as an aside to Shelby.

"Ancient history," the CRS financial officer replied.

Images of high-tech workshops where T-1 battlefield robots were being readied for service came up on the screen. Scientists and technicians in white lab coats used a variety of test equipment to check every system in the machines.

"T-1 and H-K research and development is complete," the narrator reported. "On budget, ahead of schedule."

Rows of T-1s ready for action were moving into holding areas.

"Working prototypes are now up and running, ready to face action in the conflicts of tomorrow."

Suddenly the video image cut to a military funeral on a bleak, overcast day. A coffin was draped in an American flag.

"Today, the loss of even one soldier in combat is intolerable—ask your constituents."

The video image switched to a chart that showed the evolution of robotics from the first primitive factory machines to the T-1s, to the skeletal Terminators, and finally to cybernetic figures in full battle armor and infiltration coverings.

"But with sufficient funding we need no longer risk the well-being of our men and women in uniform," the narrator promised. "Robots will take their place on the front lines."

The image cut to a lab where an extremely well-muscled athletic man with narrow hips, broad shoulders, and powerful legs was running on a treadmill. He was dressed only in Spandex shorts. Sensors were placed all over his body, which glistened with sweat. Doctors and medical techs monitored the man's progress.

"Motion capture studies are being applied even now to the development of the next generation of robotic defense systems," the narrator said.

In an inset an animated steel robot mimicked the human test subject's motions.

The camera moved to the front of the athlete who stepped off the treadmill and wiped his square, ruggedly cut handsome face with a towel.

The new cybernetic systems were being called Terminators, Brewster thought. This one, the T-600, with a similar model, the T-800, in development.

"I'm Chief Master Sergeant William Candy," the athlete model said, his Texas drawl thick. "I was honored to be selected in the ongoing effort to save American lives."

Brewster frowned. He hadn't seen this part before. He glanced over at Shelby's assistant running the video. The man had been responsible for much of the production work. "Laying it on a little thick, wouldn't you say?"

"It's a sales tool, General," Olson replied.

"I don't know about that accent," Shelby groused.

"We can fix it, sir," his assistant assured him.

Brewster's chief engineer, Tony Flickinger, came into the presentation room and went to his boss.

"Systems are crashing all over the place," he said in Brewster's ear so that no one else could hear him. "I don't know if we can stop it."

Brewster got up, his heart skipping a beat, his stomach tied in a knot.

Shelby looked up, puzzled, even a little angry by the interruption. "Bob?"

"Sorry, something important," Brewster said.

"What could be more important than this?" Shelby asked. The video image on the screen was on pause. The others in the room didn't look happy either. "Budget hearings start next week. If we don't land the production contract—"

"You'll have to excuse me," Brewster said, and he left with his chief engineer.

"That man will not focus," Shelby's assistant muttered, and he hit the remote to continue the video presentation.

Sergeant Candy was in uniform. He stood beside the skeleton of a nonfunctioning Terminator.

"It's now within our power to make war *safe*," Candy said. "And that truly is priceless."

The image cut to an injection mold from which the shell of a head had been formed. There were no teeth, no eyes, no flesh tones, but it was the face of Sergeant Candy.

"CRS brings you the face of the future," Candy said.

Above the Mojave

As they crested Soledad Pass and started down into the desert, Kate tried the dash-mounted cell phone again to see if she could get through to her father.

She got a dial tone, but after the first three numbers, the signal strength faded and dropped to zero.

Thirty seconds later it was back. She cleared the keypad and tried again. This time after only one number the phone received a series of squeals and warbling tones as if a computer were trying to connect with them.

It was frustrating to her. And frightening not only because of what might happen to her father if the T-X got to him first, but also because of the chaos in everything else that seemed to be going on.

Last night she would not have believed any of what she had gone through this morning was possible. Nor had it been conceivable to her that the world was on the brink of all-out nuclear war. Global thermonuclear war. The ultimate sword of Damocles.

Now she wasn't so sure of anything. Least of all her

own senses. This had to be a dream. Yet she knew that it was not.

She broke the connection and replaced the cell phone on its bracket. "The whole cell network's down," she said.

She sat in the Winnebago's passenger seat. Terminator drove and John was at the dinette table in back putting fuses into blocks of C-4 explosive.

They were heading north out of the mountains, Edwards Air Force Base less than thirty miles away.

Terminator glanced at her. "Skynet is assuming control of global communications, in preparation for its attack," he said.

She was still having trouble buying into the entire scenario. But she had to ask the next question, no matter how crazy it sounded in her own ears.

"So—if this is a war between people and machines, why are you on our side?"

"The resistance captured me and reprogrammed my CPU," Terminator said blandly. He could have been discussing the weather. "I was originally designed for assassination missions."

Like the T-X model, Kate thought with a shudder. "Does that bother you now?"

"Remorse is a human concept based on the illusion of free will. It has no meaning to me."

"So you don't really *care* if this mission succeeds or not," Kate said. She looked back at Connor who was watching them. "If we get killed, would *that* mean anything to you?"

Terminator seemed to give her question serious consideration. "If you were to die, then I would become useless," he answered. "There would be no reason for me to exist."

Kate had to turn away, her eyes wanted to fill. "Thank you for doing this," she said softly.

"Your gratitude is not required," Terminator told her indifferently. "I am programmed to follow your commands."

Connor was suddenly very interested. "Her commands?" he asked.

Terminator glanced at his reflection in the inside mirror. "It was Katherine Brewster who had me reactivated and sent through the time displacement field."

Kate held up a hand. "What exactly am I in this future of yours?"

Terminator turned to her. "You are John Connor's spouse and second-in-command."

Kate was shocked, though she knew that she shouldn't be. Nothing should be surprising to her ever again. She turned back to take a good look at Connor. Her future husband, if Terminator could be believed.

"Don't look at me, it's not my idea," he told her.

Kate continued to stare at him. She tried to remember what it had been like in Kripke's basement, making out with him. Although she remembered his face, she was fuzzy on the details of what exactly they had done.

She shook her head slowly. "No way."

Connor was obviously stung. "What?"

"You're a mess," Kate told him.

Connor shook his head and grinned wryly. "You're

not exactly my type either," he said. He turned to Terminator. "Why didn't *I* send you back?" he asked.

"I am not authorized to answer your question."

"Right," Connor said. "You ask him," he told Kate.

"Why didn't *he* send you back?" Kate asked.

"He was dead," Terminator answered.

It was another hammer blow to Kate's already bruised emotions. Terminator seemed to be indifferent to the impact of what he had told them. To him it was just another dry bit of data. But Connor had been affected. That much was obvious.

"Oh, that sucks," he said, trying to make light of it.

"Humans inevitably die," Terminator said reasonably.

"Yeah, I know," Connor said. "How does it—" He shook his head. "Maybe I don't want to know."

"How does he die?" Kate asked.

"John Connor was terminated on July fourth, 2032," Terminator said. "I was selected for the emotional attachment he felt to my model number, due to his boyhood experiences. This aided in my infiltration."

"What are you saying?" Connor asked.

Terminator did not take his eyes off the road. "I killed you," he said.

Edwards Air Force Base

"Edwards Air Force Base, this is LAPD helicopter, Nancy-one-zero-zero-niner, inbound. Request permission to land," T-X radioed.

Staff Sergeant Gloria Sanchez raised her binoculars and studied the sky to the west. The helicopter was too low for radar. She spotted the dark blue LAPD chopper low out of the sun. She keyed her mike.

"LAPD, Nancy-one-zero-zero-niner, this is Edwards Control Tower. What can we do for you this afternoon?"

"I'm probably on a wild goose chase, Edwards, but we're looking for a kidnapping suspect," T-X radioed pleasantly in a man's voice. She wore the dark blue jumpsuit and LAPD badge of Sergeant Ricco, the pilot. "The suspect may be headed out this way. I was wondering if I could talk to someone from security. I have photos. And you guys are about the only people I can raise right now."

"We're having problems with our comms too, zero-niner. Stand by." She telephoned the OD at Base Security, Captain McManus.

"Have him set down on the flight line, in front of 2004," the captain said. "I'll send someone over to talk to him."

"Yes, sir," Sanchez said. She got on the radio. "Zero-niner, Edwards. You have permission to land. Pressure is two-niner-point-niner-seven. Winds out of zero-eight-five at eight knots."

"Roger that," T-X radioed. "Where would you like me to set down?"

"On the flight line, just east of the tower. We'll have someone with wands to show you where."

"Much obliged," T-X said.

"My pleasure, zero-niner."

CRS

General Brewster moved en masse with Tony Flickinger and several of his senior engineers down the tech country corridor to the Computer Center.

It was business as usual here, except on the global net where, according to his people, everything was falling apart like a house of cards. Nothing they tried seemed to work.

"There has to be a mistake," Brewster said, his stomach sour. He couldn't remember if he'd eaten lunch. "As of fifteen hundred hours, all primary military systems were secure."

The hallway went through the Research & Development wing; glassed-in tech areas and clean rooms where some of their cutting-edge work was being done. Scientists and engineers in white suits, paper caps and booties, and respirators operated a wide range of remote manipulators, electronic test equipment, and biohazard glove boxes. The latest cybernetic prototypes were being put together here.

The people behind the glass walls, enclosed in their

hermetic spaces, seemed oblivious to the mounting chaos outside. But they were the purists, Brewster thought. They were the creators of the individual bits and pieces, so they did not have to worry about the whole.

The environment was comfortable for them. CRS made sure of it.

"They were secure," one of the senior engineers said. Brewster couldn't recall his name. "Only the civilian sector was affected—the Internet, air traffic, power plants, that sort of thing."

"But then?" Brewster prompted.

"But then a few minutes ago we got word that guidance computers at Vandenburg crashed."

"We thought it was a communications error," one of the other senior engineers said. Brewster thought his name might be Tobias.

"But?" Brewster asked. There were always buts in this business.

"Now it looks like the virus," Tobias admitted.

Flickinger wore a headset that connected him to the mainframe. He pressed the earpiece a little tighter. They were even starting to have trouble with internal communications. "Early warning in Alaska is down," he said.

Brewster stopped in midstride. "Why?" This wasn't happening.

"Signals from half our satellites are scrambled beyond recognition," another of the engineers said.

"What about our missile silos, our submarines?" Brewster demanded.

"We've lost contact," Tobias said.

To the engineers this was merely a problem in systems integration; a technical glitch, a problem that in the aircraft industry was called an unk-unk. An unknown-unknown. Troubles were certain to pop up in the start-up of any complicated system. And most of them were expected. But there were always the few problems that no one could predict. Except to predict that they would occur.

They were the unk-unks, which were happening this moment with the worldwide network of communications systems; what the military called Technical Means.

"Dear God. You're saying that the country is completely open to attack?" Brewster demanded.

His chief engineer glanced at the others, and nodded. "Theoretically we could be under attack already, and we wouldn't know it."

"Who's doing this? A foreign power? Or is it some teenage hacker in his garage?"

Flickinger shook his head. He was at a loss. "We can't trace the virus. We can't pin it down."

"It's like nothing we've ever seen," Tobias added. "It keeps growing. Changing. Like it's got a mind of its own."

Brewster moved to the glass wall of the Power Lab. A humanoid torso, its chest open to reveal a pair of power units and a maze of electronic circuitry and servos, was set up on a test stand. A white-coated lab tech was taking a reading on a frequency spectrum analyzer. Wires snaked from several pieces of test equipment to the cybernetic device.

To the technician doing his work this afternoon everything was crystal clear. They all were on overtime, but sooner or later he would go home, perhaps to a wife and children. A cold beer, a shower, dinner, and afterward lovemaking. Brewster felt far removed from that sort of a simple existence. With each star that had been pinned on his shoulders, he'd taken a giant step away from any kind of a normal life.

"I don't understand," he said to his engineers. "This can't be happening."

Watching the lab tech work, Brewster wondered if he would trade with the man right now; even up, life-for-life. But he didn't have the answer. It wasn't that simple.

"Sir, the Pentagon's on the secure line," Flickinger said. "It's the chairman."

Brewster tore his eyes away from the lab tech, and nodded. "All right."

At the end of the corridor they went through double doors into the two-story open Computer Center that took up the entire end of the R&D wing. Dozens of technicians and operators, some of them military, some of them civilian, worked at computer consoles scattered throughout the big room. Many of them worked in open quad cubicles, while others worked in the Mainframe Control Center behind glass partitions. There were no windows in the room, only the louvers of large air-conditioning vents.

There was a hum of feverish activity here this afternoon that wasn't normal. Blinking warning lights, hurried telephone conversations as operators tried to reestablish communications, flashing computer screens, error messages all warning that the global net was in the process of totally collapsing.

Brewster strode directly over to one of the duty officer's positions, snatched the red secure phone, and punched the blinking encrypt light.

"Brewster," he barked. His engineers and several of the techs gathered around him to find out what was going on.

Admiral James F. Morrison, chairman of the Joint Chiefs of Staff, was on the line. "We're hoping to hell you've got some kind of solution for us," he shouted. He was angrier than Brewster had ever heard him. And the admiral was well known for his short fuse.

"I know what you're looking for, sir, but Skynet is not ready for a system-wide connection," Brewster said.

Washington had been pressuring him to at least bring Skynet on-line. All the high-tech weapons and other toys could wait. But Skynet was ready now, at least it was in the estimation of a lot of congressional and Beltway insiders. And that included Admiral Morrison. Brewster was damned if he didn't and damned by a different but no less powerful contingent if he did.

"That's not what your civilian counterparts over there just told me," Morrison railed. "They're telling me that whiz-bang project I just spent fifteen billion dollars on can stop this damn virus."

"Sir, there are other steps that we should consider first—"

"Bob, I don't have *time* for that," Morrison countered.

"I've got nuke boats and silos, and I don't know what the hell messages this virus is sending them."

Brewster glanced at his people and shook his head. He was on the losing side of this argument.

"I understand there's a certain amount of performance anxiety over there, but your boys are saying that if we plug Skynet into all our systems, it'll squash this thing like a bug and give me back control of my military."

It had to be Shelby talking to the admiral. But Shelby was only a bean counter.

"Mr. Chairman, I need to be real clear about this," Brewster started. He would try one last time to get Morrison to slow down and think it out. "If we uplink now, Skynet will be in control of the military."

"But you'll be in control of Skynet, right?" the admiral shot back.

"That's correct," Brewster answered cautiously.

"Then do it," Morrison ordered. "And, Bob? This thing works, you got all the funding you ever need."

"Yes, sir," Brewster said. He slowly replaced the red phone on its cradle.

He stood for a moment, thinking it out. The nets were all crashing, so uplinking to Skynet could in itself be problematic.

But, and this was a very large but in his mind, if they could uplink with Skynet, and the system took out the virus, could they just as easily shut it down?

Skynet was nothing short of tenacious, and ingenious. It had been designed to think for itself; to adapt to any and all threats against it.

Brewster wondered when all was said and done if Skynet would consider *them* a threat.

He turned to his people. "Okay. Set it up," he ordered.

"Yes, General," Patricia Talbot replied. She was a CRS systems chief tech. A sharp woman.

She strode across the room to the Mainframe Control Center, issuing orders like a destroyer captain taking her ship into battle.

Mojave Desert

The big green highway sign said EDWARDS AFB. ROSA-
MOND GATE. 11 MILES. A hundred yards later they passed
a sign that said EXIT 6. LANCASTER. QUARTZ HILL. 1 MILE.

"Turn here," Kate told Terminator.

So far no one had come after them. The sky was clear
of police helicopters, and traffic was very light on the
interstate.

Kate had tried twice more to reach her father, with
the same results as earlier. The cell phone networks were
down. Even the radio didn't work, especially on FM, although she'd been able to pick up something that
sounded like music in the very faint distance on AM.

Terminator got off the interstate and headed east
across the desert. There were three ways onto Edwards:
the Rosamond Gate off I-14, the North Gate off Highway
58, and the South Gate at the southeastern extremity of
Rogers Dry Lake.

The South Gate was the least used entrance for the
air base itself, but was the primary entrance for the CRS
Research & Development facility.

Edwards was a large place, more than five hundred square miles in which a lot of black projects, including CRS, had been and continued to be hidden from the public's view.

Kate had been out here only twice before; once at a ribbon-cutting ceremony for CRS. That was before she started college, and before her parents' divorce. There hadn't been many family members at the opening, and Kate remembered how proud she'd been of her father. He'd just received his second star, and to her he'd seemed to be twenty feet tall that day.

The second time she'd come out here was last year when she'd talked to her father about her engagement to Scott. Her mother had been all for the marriage, but she'd always been her daddy's girl, and she'd desperately wanted his approval.

Which he'd given. But she'd not seen him since, not once. They talked on the phone, but he was always too busy to come into L.A., even for a weekend.

She glanced back at Connor, who was still working on getting the explosives ready. By the looks of it he meant to destroy the entire complex. But he had no idea how big the place was.

When he'd started making suggestions how to get onto the base, Kate had cut him off. "I'll take care of that part," she told him.

He'd exchanged a glance with Terminator, but then nodded and went back to his work.

"About ten miles and there'll be a sign for Cyber Research," she told Terminator. She got up and went to where Connor was stuffing bricks of C-4 into satchels, and sat down across from him.

There seemed to be weapons and ammunition, rockets, grenades, explosives everywhere. She shook her head. "This is so . . ." She was at a loss. "God, there isn't even a word for what this is."

"Yeah," Connor said. He fastened the flap of a satchel and set it aside. "Look, none of it's going to happen. We get your dad, pull the plug on Skynet, and the bombs won't fall." He nodded toward Terminator, driving. "He won't have to kill me someday. He'll never even exist."

Terminator looked up at them in the interior mirror, but said nothing. The rolling desert hills were bleak, almost like a moonscape.

"And you and me," Connor said. "We can go our separate ways."

Kate was confused. She didn't know how to take what John was telling her. She looked out the window at the passing desert, her thoughts drifting back to when she was a kid. She had to smile.

She turned back to Connor. "You know Mike Kripke's basement? That was the first time I ever kissed a guy."

"Really," Connor said, grinning. "Now *that's* weird."

Kate returned his grin, and they both laughed a little.

Terminator glanced at their reflection. "Your levity is good," he said solemnly. "It relieves tension and the fear of death."

Connor gave a derisive snort, shook his head, and sat back. The up mood had evaporated in an instant.

CRS

A pretty young first lieutenant whose name tag read HASTINGS got off an elevator one floor below the Computer Center and headed down the broad, well-lit corridor as if she were on a mission.

There was a sense of urgency throughout the complex. Worldwide communications were failing, military networks were crashing, and a lot of the people here whose job it was to see that such things did not happen were in a near panic.

Hastings was blond, slender, and attractive in her Air Force blue cotton blouse and dark blue skirt. Halfway down the corridor she stopped at a door that was marked by a placard:

> ### CRS
> #### T-1 STORAGE BAY 3
> Please make sure T-1 unit power charge
> connection is complete and secure at
> hook-up point for proper charge transference.

The corridor was empty of people for the moment. Hastings tried the door, but it was locked. She turned the handle past its stop, snapping the lock pins as if they were matchsticks.

Checking again to make sure she had not been observed, she slipped into the large, dimly lit room and closed the door behind her.

Row upon row of large, plastic-shrouded figures were packed into the storage bay. T-X hesitated only a moment to study the sensor readouts in her head-up display, before she ripped the plastic off the first T-1 robot and tossed it aside.

The index finger of her left hand morphed into a long, slender drill bit that she used to enter the warrior robot's tiny skull case.

A millisecond later her fingertip glowed blue with plasma energy and she transferred a stream of data into the T-1's processor.

Finished almost as quickly as she had begun, T-X withdrew her data probe and moved to the next robot in line.

Edwards South Gate

Both times Kate had been out here the CRS complex had come as something of a surprise to her. First there was nothing but desert; rolling sand hills, scrub brush, Joshua trees. Then, over the crest of a low hill the complex was suddenly spread out in the distance.

Protected by a double row of razor wire, the gate manned by serious-looking armed Air Force Security Police, the main Research & Development facility was housed in an ultramodern three-story glass and steel building that bristled with satellite dishes, laser guidance transmission heads, and its own separate power station and air-conditioning plant.

Some distance behind the rambling building from which a dozen different wings branched in all directions was the antennae farm for worldwide communications and data links from the upper gigahertz frequency range all the way down to ELF—Extremely Low Frequencies—used for communications with submarines.

In the basement and subbasement levels were beehives of laboratories where sensitive experiments took place around the clock. Beneath the hangars and stretching in a huge circle nearly a half mile in diameter was a super-cooled particle accelerator, the electromagnets of which in themselves constituted a radiation hazard when operating at full power.

An airstrip ran east and west with a modern control tower and several hangars and maintenance buildings nearby. Several military transport aircraft, a number of helicopters, and several small private aircraft were parked on the ramp or inside the hangars.

Terminator spotted the LAPD helicopter in front of one of the hangars.

"T-X is already here," he said.

Kate scrambled to the passenger seat as they started down the long hill to the gate, still a half mile away. "How do you know?" she demanded, her heart in her throat.

"The police helicopter. N-one-zero-zero-nine. It was in the air near the cemetery." Terminator pointed to the chopper on the ramp.

"Oh, God," Kate said. "Hurry." She turned to Connor. "Cover up that stuff. I'm going to talk our way onto the base."

Connor grabbed a blanket and covered the weapons and explosives as Terminator slowed for the gate.

A pair of Air Policemen stepped out and motioned for Terminator to stop. He pulled up and opened the side window. Kate leaned across to talk to the security cops.

"I'm Kate Brewster. My dad, General Brewster, is expecting us," she said.

The security officers were dressed in BDUs with black berets, M16s slung over their shoulders. "May I see some identification, please?" the tech sergeant asked.

Kate took her driver's license out of the wallet in her jacket pocket and handed it down. "My fiancé, Scott Peterson, is in back," she said. She smiled and placed a hand on Terminator's arm. "This is . . . Tom Peterson . . . his brother. Our best man."

The sergeant went into the guardhouse with Kate's ID, while the other guard kept a watchful eye on them. There was no traffic.

A couple of minutes later the sergeant came out and handed Kate's driver's license back. "The general's a little busy right now, ma'am. But his secretary's authorized your visit."

The second guard swung the gate open.

"Straight ahead to the main entrance," the sergeant instructed. "Someone will meet you there and get you signed in."

"Thank you," Kate said. "Please hurry," she said under her breath to Terminator.

CRS Computer Center

CRS was at the highest state of readiness it had ever been. There was an air not so much of panic, but of expectation. Awe. A little trepidation.

General Brewster stood next to the Mainframe Duty Officer's console, looking up at the display on the large plasma screen on the back wall.

The field was deep blue, a Mercator projection of the western hemisphere centered on the North and South American continents, with the shoulder of Africa off to the right and the Pacific out to Guam to the left.

U.S. air, naval, and ground stations were highlighted by icons, the electronic networks connecting them marked by lines, along with the great circle flying and sailing routes to battle zones.

The display was labeled SKYNET BATTLEFIELD MANAGEMENT SYSTEM. Tool bars were labeled FIREWALL PENETRATION. LOCAL DEFENSE NETS. SYSTEM STATUS.

In rapid succession every military network, base, unit, or weapons system currently en route came up with an ON-LINE icon.

At the end of the list was the simple interrogative: Y/N.

The big room quieted down by degrees as the last of the installations came on-line.

Skynet was telling its human controllers that it was ready. It was asking if they were ready too.

Tony Flickinger was at Brewster's elbow. "Sir, shall I?"

Brewster shook his head. "No. It's my job now." He had trouble dragging his eyes from the display. He hesitated.

This was what they all had worked for over the past several years. This was what the Pentagon had spent more than fifteen billion dollars on. Actually more had been spent, but the above-the-line budget, the number that Congress saw, was fifteen billion.

Skynet was going to assure world peace. No national leader in his or her right mind would dare attack when such an efficient, emotionless, capable system stood watch, unblinking twenty-four/seven.

Attack the U.S. or one of her allies and die. Simple. All the power of the mightiest nation on earth would be unleashed.

An unstoppable force.

Worldwide domination—benevolent domination— was possible for the first time in the history of man.

Still Brewster hesitated. Maybe Mr. Watchdog— Congressman Stevenson—was right. Maybe turning over our entire defense network to a goddamn computer was nuts.

But they had run out of options. The U.S. and her allies were, because of the virus, totally defenseless at this moment.

Brewster reached out, almost languidly, and touched

the Y key on the Mainframe DO's console, and a moment later ENTER.

The console monitor brought up the CRS logo, and the message SKYNET LINK ESTABLISHED.

The system began to shift and change, slowly at first, but rapidly accelerating as tens of thousands of Skynet links were established worldwide.

"We're in," one of the techs at a computer console announced. "We're past the firewalls. Local defense nets, minutemen, subs—"

It was moving too fast now for the technician to keep up with it verbally.

"Skynet is fully operational," another of the techs reported. "Processing at sixty—now ninety teraflops a second—"

"Sir, it should take less than a minute to find the virus and kill it," Patricia Talbot advised.

Brewster glanced at the systems chief tech. He didn't know if he shared her optimism. "Let's pray to God it works," he said.

The plasma screen and every terminal in the Mainframe Center and out in the main room suddenly went blank.

It was as if someone had pulled the switch.

Brewster looked up, his heart in his mouth. "What the—?"

"Power failure?" someone asked.

"Lights are still on," someone else observed.

The monitors and the plasma screen suddenly came back to life, and for a few seconds Brewster breathed a sigh of relief. Skynet had merely been clearing its throat.

But then it became obvious that something very wrong was happening. The screens and monitors were filling with line after line of some alien code, symbols racing across the videos at inhuman speeds.

"What the hell is going on—" Brewster muttered. What indeed.

CRS

T-X was ready to move now; the last of the operational robots on the floor had been reprogrammed.

The door to T-1 Storage Bay 3 opened, and Lieutenant Hastings stepped out into the corridor just as her boss Captain McManus got off the elevator.

He was angry, and the moment he spotted her he charged down the hall like a bull on the rampage.

"Lieutenant, where in hell did you go?" he demanded. "Where in hell is that police chopper pilot? And—" He glanced at the placard on the door. "What in hell are you doing here?"

"How did you know I was here?" T-X asked without inflection.

"Jones spotted you—"

"Who else knows?" T-X asked.

Something suddenly occurred to McManus, and he stepped closer. "Say, you're not Hastings." He looked again at the placard. "Who the hell—?"

T-X grabbed him by the throat and lifted him off his feet. Opening the door to the T-1 Storage Bay she shook him like a rag doll, breaking the vertebrae in his neck. She took his sidearm and tossed him in a corner.

T-X stared at the dying captain for a moment, only his left leg still twitching, considering taking his persona to more easily reach the Computer Center.

She looked up, her sensors attuned to the electronic emissions inside the building. There was a powerful interference here, strong electrical and electronic sources that dulled some of her sensors.

But she could feel that Skynet was coming on-line now, and very soon it would be next to impossible to shut it down.

She cocked her head. *Next* to impossible. But there was still a way to do it. General Brewster was the key.

She turned without another glance at the chief of security and headed to the elevator as she began to morph out of her Lieutenant Hastings persona.

A pair of Air Force security guards were stationed inside a bulletproof glass partition just past the front door.

"Where would your father be if there was trouble with the system?" Terminator asked Kate.

"Upstairs in the Computer Center," Kate told him. Her father had said that was the heart of CRS. But now that they had come this far she didn't know what to do the rest of the way.

"Do you know how to reach the Computer Center?"

Kate nodded. "Yes." She nodded toward the elevators

across the lobby from them. "But they won't let us go up there—"

One of the security guards slid a clipboard through the slot. "Please sign in," he said pleasantly. "Someone will be out in just a minute to escort you upstairs to the general's office."

"We're going now," Terminator said. He smashed the thick glass with his left fist, and shot both guards in the knee with a Glock pistol, dropping them to the floor with yelps of pain.

"What . . . are you crazy?" Kate shouted.

"There is no time," Terminator told her. "We must reach your father."

He strode off to the elevator, while Connor took Kate's arm and followed after him.

"He's been programmed not to kill people," Connor assured her. "Doesn't mean he can't disable them."

All their terminals were locked out.

General Brewster emerged from the Mainframe room out onto the Computer Center floor. His technicians were scrambling to regain control of the system. Doing everything they could to take back just one base, one military installation. Any satellite.

But even the CRS complex power station and air-conditioning plant were no longer responding. Nor were internal communications, including telephones, working.

One of the techs who had been trying to get through

to a friend on the other side of Edwards looked up and shook his head. "Cell phones are all down too, sir."

The only ray of hope in the entire mess was the virus they had been plagued with. Skynet was eliminating it, although it was taking more than the one minute that Talbot had promised.

But at what cost?

No one knew how long this situation would last, or where it was going.

"Daddy?" a woman getting off the service elevator at the back of the center shouted.

Brewster knew that voice. He turned on his heel as his daughter, Kate, came across the room toward him, her right hand extended as if she wanted to come into his arms and be held.

But her being here now, at this moment, made no sense. Then he suddenly remembered that he had asked her to bring her fiancé out today. Practically begged her, and he told his secretary to take care of security if and when she actually did show up.

But not now.

"Kate, honey, what are you doing here?"

The main elevator to Brewster's left opened and he saw several people out of the corner of his eye coming toward him.

He started to turn when machine-gun fire erupted, the noise shockingly loud. One part of his brain automatically registered the fact that the gun was a Russian AK-47. They had a distinctive sound.

Another part of his brain reacted in horror as Kate's body was hammered with bullets.

She was shoved backward, crashing through a partition in a shower of glass, computers exploding in sparks and plastic and metal shards, Kate falling to the floor in a heap behind a console.

Pandemonium erupted as technicians dove for cover, screaming in panic, trying to get out of the line of fire.

This was some kind of a nightmare. All the air had gone out of the room, and Brewster could not breathe, let alone cry out his daughter's name.

He started forward when a woman to his left shouted at him.

"Get away from it!"

It was Kate. He would know her voice anywhere. Behind him. But he could see her feet on the other side of the destroyed console where she had fallen.

He turned in time to see his daughter coming toward him in a dead run. A young man in torn, bloody blue jeans and a scuffed-up suede jacket, a knapsack over his shoulder, came right behind her. He carried an AK-47.

A large man, vaguely familiar, dressed in black leather, sunglasses covering his eyes, strode across the room. He dropped the AK-47 he'd just fired and unslung a Mk-19 grenade launcher from his right shoulder.

A mass exodus out of the two emergency exits was taking place as technicians scrambled, some of them on all fours, to get out of what had become a battle zone.

Kate was coming across the room toward Brewster,

but that was impossible. He'd seen his daughter hit at least a half-dozen times and fall to the floor,

He turned again in time to see a bullet-riddled figure rise up from behind the computer console quad. It was Kate, and yet it wasn't.

Brewster staggered back a half step with the enormity of what he was witnessing.

There was no blood. Something that looked like liquid metal was coalescing around the wounds, closing them, impossibly healing her injuries.

But she wasn't Kate now. She was a blond woman dressed in rust-colored pants and a jacket.

T-X raised the Beretta 9mm pistol she'd taken from Captain McManus's body, and fired two shots, both slamming into Brewster's stomach, shoving him back as if he'd been hit by a freight train coming at full speed.

Kate screamed.

At that moment Terminator fired the first 40mm grenade, hitting T-X squarely in the chest with a tremendous explosion that shoved her back several steps, almost off her feet.

But she recovered, and had taken a step forward when Terminator fired a second grenade at her, which hit her chest again, shoving her backward.

Not waiting for her to recover, Terminator fired again as he moved toward her. Each time she was pushed back several feet by the force of the blast. And each time before she could regain her forward momentum from the attack, Terminator fired again.

With the last grenade T-X was pushed back into the

broad louvers over the main ventilation shaft that shattered from her weight. She disappeared through the opening.

Alarms were ringing, sirens shrieking as technicians continued to get out of the Computer Center as fast as they could move.

Kate raced to her father's side. He was spitting up blood, and obviously was in great pain. He could not talk above a whisper as Kate set to work checking the extent of his wounds.

"Katie, thank God. I thought—"

"Don't talk, Daddy," she said. She opened his blood-soaked blouse and shirt. Black fluid leaked out of one of his belly wounds. He had to be taken to a hospital soon or he would die.

Terminator walked over to the busted open ventilator shaft and looked inside. It ran straight down for a couple of stories, ending at the shattered blades of a large fan.

Terminator turned to Connor and Kate. "She'll be back," he told them.

Connor nodded grimly. He hunched down beside Kate and her father. "We have to shut down Skynet," he told the general. "Where's the system core, somewhere in this building?"

Brewster had trouble digesting what the young man was telling him. It wasn't possible. "Who are you?" he whispered, the words gurgling in his throat. "You can't know about that."

Connor grabbed his shoulder. "Cut the top-secret shit!"

Kate batted his hand away. "Stop," she screamed. "You're hurting him!"

Connor turned on her. "If he can't tell us what we need to know, we're all dead." He grabbed a handful of Brewster's uniform blouse. "Where is it? How can you shut it down?"

"Skynet," Brewster mumbled breathlessly. "It's fighting the virus."

Connor took a breath. His eyes never left the General's. "You don't understand, do you? Skynet *is* the virus," Connor shouted over the noise of the alarms and sirens. "It's the reason everything's falling apart."

This was even more impossible to believe than anything else. "No, that can't be true," Brewster croaked. "I just gave the command to . . . link to all secure military systems."

Terminator came over, reloading the grenade launcher. He'd retrieved the AK-47 and he slapped a magazine into its receiver.

"Skynet has become self-aware," he said. "In one hour it will initiate a massive nuclear attack on its enemy."

Brewster looked up. He knew this man. "What enemy?" he whispered urgently. He had to know what was happening.

"Us," Connor said with bitter finality.

There was automatic weapons fire from somewhere in the distance, but still within the building. Whatever kind of a weapon was being used, it sounded extremely fast and powerful.

People started to scream, desperate sounds rising out of the stairwells from the floor below.

Kate looked up. "Oh, God—"

"It's the machines," Connor said. "They're starting to take over."

Brewster reached up and grasped Connor's arm, finally realizing that this was no nightmare. The young man was right.

"My private office," he said with great difficulty. "On this floor. We have to get there. The access codes, they're in the safe."

Between Connor and Kate they managed to get the general to his feet.

Terminator led the way as advance guard, his AK-47 and Mk-19 up and at the ready.

CRS

Brewster directed them toward the corridor to the right that led, he said, to his office and the offices of the principal engineers and administrators.

The entire building was in a panic now. They could hear gunfire from every direction, some of which was the sharper sounds of the M16s the Air Force security troops carried.

But the guards were outclassed by the chainguns the robots were equipped with.

Just as they were leaving the Computer Center, they looked back in time to see the main elevator doors opening. A group of eight or ten technicians sprang up from behind consoles meaning to scramble aboard the elevator and get away.

But a T-1 robot, massive on its twin treads, its red optical sensors in the tiny cranial case ominous, its bulk almost completely filling the elevator car, immediately opened fire with its twin chainguns. The depleted uranium slugs tore into the people, ripping their bodies apart, blood and shattered bones flying outward like geysers.

Terminator stepped around the corner and had started down the corridor, his weapons at the ready.

Connor and Kate half carried, half dragged the general out of the Computer Center, moving as quickly as they could.

Kate's heart pounded nearly out of her chest as they held up at a corner. Terminator took a quick look, then stepped out across the empty corridor.

"What was that?" Kate asked.

Terminator glanced back at her. "A T-1, first generation terminator. Primitive targeting system, heat and motion sensitive."

Brewster suddenly struggled to get his balance. To stand on his own two feet. "You're Sergeant Candy," he blurted.

Terminator took a quick look up the still empty corridor, then turned back. Brewster's eyes widened. A small section of Terminator's metal cranial case was exposed.

"Negative," Terminator answered.

"Jesus—where did you come from?"

"I was built here," Terminator said.

A sudden burst of chaingun fire in the vicinity of the conference room to their left sent them hurrying down the corridor.

They could hear more screams now, and crashing sounds; shrieking metal, breaking glass, sporadic return fire from the Air Force security people.

Brewster could not understand how Skynet had taken

over the entire system so quickly, but he was even more confused about the T-1 robots. Someone had reprogrammed them, or at the very least was controlling their actions.

But how? And why? What was the purpose behind all this? There had to be reasons.

Ultimately, however, all of this was his fault. He had been the driving force behind integrating CRS research and development results in the military structure.

Skynet and its control of all U.S. forces and weapons systems had been his passion from the beginning.

He had earned his first star when he had straightened out the mess left by the destruction and bankruptcy of the old Cyberdyne company. His second star came when this CRS facility was opened six years ago. And his third star was added six months ago when the major work on Skynet had been completed.

He was tired. He wanted to lie down and go to sleep. He missed Kate's mother, and he missed a normal life that he'd never had.

He turned and looked at his daughter, a wave of love welling up inside of him.

"Kate, I'm sorry," he whispered. "I'm so sorry."

"Sssh, it's not your fault," she told him. Her face was screwed up in fear and worry.

"It is. I opened Pandora's box," Brewster said. He glanced at Connor. "You did the right thing, Katie."

"What?" She was having a hard time focusing on what he was trying to tell her, while still maintaining the pace behind Terminator.

"Your fiancé," Brewster said. "He's a good man."

Connor gave Kate a brief smile. Brewster could see that they were a team. It was a good sign.

Terminator pulled up short at another intersecting corridor and immediately stepped back. He motioned for them to keep quiet and then laid his weapons on the floor.

Brewster looked over at the glass partition to one of the offices. He could see the hazy reflection of a T-1 robot at the end of the intersecting corridor.

It remained there, motionless. Its sensors were trained down the corridor in their direction. It might have heard or detected something, but it wasn't certain.

Terminator was seeing the same reflection.

A second T-1 robot trundled around the corner and stopped next to the first unit.

Terminator motioned for Connor, Kate, and her father to keep very still, then he reached up and silently removed a foam-core panel from the false ceiling. Above, in the four-foot crawl space, were the hangers for the ceiling tiles and channels, the lights and the wiring for the closed circuit security cameras at every intersection, and the electronic and optic fiber runs in sheet-metal ducts.

Terminator pulled himself up into the crawl space with impossible ease, and then, moving hand over hand along the cable runs, disappeared into the darkness.

He was one of the advanced cyborg warrior robots modeled after Sergeant Candy. Brewster was certain of it. But what was so confusing to him was that the Sergeant

Candy terminator model wasn't operational yet.

Where did this one come from?

Kate and Connor spotted the reflection in the glass partition. They stood stock still as one of the T-1 robots moved a few feet up the corridor.

It was obvious that the machine sensed something. Possibly their heat signatures from around the corner.

It moved forward a couple more feet.

Connor started to pull Kate and her father back, when a ceiling panel directly behind the second T-1 burst open and Terminator dropped out of the crawl space like a Special Forces paratrooper landing in enemy-held territory.

Both T-1 robots immediately swiveled toward the movement, bringing their weapons to bear.

Keeping one step behind the second T-1, Terminator wrenched its cranial case off its blunt torso, then grabbed the barrel of the unit's chaingun as it started to fire.

The first T-1 opened fire down the corridor, but Terminator used the second unit as a shield, forcing its shorted chaingun to bear on the first robot, firing at its cranial case where its CPU was located, and at the center of its torso where its power units were shielded.

The first T-1 fell silent, its red optical sensor winking out, the muzzles of its chainguns drooping toward the floor, a second before the unit Terminator was manipulating stopped functioning.

Both T-1s were badly shot up, and would not soon be brought back into service. Terminator cocked his head for a moment, his sensors alert for the close proximity of any other T-X controlled weapon. But his head-up display was clear.

He went back to where Connor and Kate and her father were waiting around the corner. He retrieved his weapons and they went the rest of the way to the general's office.

Brewster's secretary was gone as was everyone else in this wing. Kate and Connor helped him into his office where they eased him into a red leather club chair, across from a built-in sectional couch that was curved like a banquette. The walls were richly paneled in cherry wood, and across from a large, busy desk was a full bar set up on a built-in buffet. The American and Command flags were displayed along with pictures of WWII fighters and bombers. Large windows overlooked the tarmac and hangars.

Connor found the safe, and he looked back to Brewster for the combination.

"Thirty-two left," Brewster started.

Terminator brushed Connor aside and simply ripped the door off the safe, dropping it on the carpeted floor with a heavy thud.

Kate was looking out the window at the carnage going on below, tears in her eyes, her lips quivering. This was what hell had to be like.

Several T-1 robots like the one in the elevator and the

two they'd encountered in the corridor were on the flight line, shooting indiscriminately, killing or destroying everyone and everything they encountered. Bodies littered the ramp. Trucks and cars and aircraft were on fire, and smoke poured from some building in the distance.

"They're killing everyone," she cried. "Why?"

"To destroy any possible threat to Skynet," Terminator told her.

Connor pulled papers, envelopes, and folders out of the safe, tossing them aside. "Where are the codes?"

"Red envelope," Brewster croaked.

Connor found a large red envelope and pulled it out of the safe. He held it up so Brewster could see. "These'll shut everything down?"

Brewster remembered when Kate was born. They'd been stationed at Ramstein in Germany, and he'd raced up to the Army medical center at Vogelweh just in time.

She was so incredibly beautiful and so incredibly helpless and dependent.

"Take care of my daughter," he cried.

Kate was right there at his side. "Daddy!"

The room was getting dark. It was becoming hard to focus on anything. He felt a deepening flutter in his chest that frightened him. "Crystal Peak," he muttered. "You have to get to Crystal Peak."

"What's he saying?" Connor asked.

"Crystal Peak," Terminator said. "It's a hardened facility in the Sierra Nevada Mountains, fifty-two miles northeast. Bearing zero-one-five degrees."

"That's the system core?" Connor asked the general.

"It's your only chance," Brewster said, his voice now barely a whisper.

"Daddy," Kate pleaded. "Stay with me."

Brewster slumped back, his eyes blank, his eyelids fluttering.

The carnage on the tarmac was nearly complete. Only a few humans were left alive, and the T-1 units were on them the moment they emerged from the building. Bodies littered the ramp.

"We need to get to a plane," Connor said. But he knew that there was no way they could make it across to the hangars in the open. He stuffed the red envelope into his knapsack.

They needed another route. Some way out of the main building and across to where the planes were parked without crossing the ramp.

Connor went to the general's desk and searched for something, anything that might help them. A map, a building plan, anything.

His eyes lit on a book marked EDWARDS AIR FORCE BASE LOCATOR. He opened it to a foldout diagram of the CRS facility that showed the main R&D building plus the power station, air-conditioning plant, hangars, tower, and all the interconnecting corridors on each level.

"Okay," Connor said, racing through the diagram. "This looks like a passageway." It was marked on the third sublevel.

Terminator was at his shoulder. "The particle accelerator."

"It runs under the airfield," Connor said, trying to

make sense of what he was looking at. "There's an emergency exit here," he said, stabbing a blunt finger at a spot on the diagram. "Right by this hangar. We can follow it out."

The general took a last quiet breath and his heart stopped. Kate grabbed his uniform blouse and tried to shake him awake. But he was dead, and she knew that there was nothing she could do to bring him back. It was too late.

A Hunter-Killer aerial weapons system suddenly appeared outside the window, its rocket pods trained directly at them.

Terminator raised his AK-47. "Get down," he ordered, and opened fire.

At that moment an air-to-air missile shot from the H-K's rail, trailing a long sharp tail of fire as it came directly at the broken-out window.

CRS

Connor pulled Kate behind the general's massive desk and shoved her to the floor, shielding her body with his.

The missile exploded like an atomic bomb as it hit the window shards, instantly filling the room with blinding white light, a tremendous crash, and an intense stab of heat that singed the hair on the back of Connor's neck.

It was as if a gigantic vacuum cleaner came right behind the initial explosion, sucking up nearly everything in the room and spewing it out the window that was now a huge, gaping hole in the side of the building.

Glass and debris flew everywhere. Connor kept his head down, his arms wrapped around Kate, his body tight against hers.

But then it was over and he slowly raised himself up off her, his ears ringing from the concussion. It didn't feel as if he were injured, and as far as he could tell Kate wasn't hurt either.

Terminator had taken the brunt of the blast with his torso. He'd been shoved backward off his feet. He picked himself up, his jacket smoking, more of the artificial flesh on his face and neck burned away, exposing even larger sections of his cranial case and optical sensor sockets.

Kate suddenly pushed Connor away and half scrambled, half crawled over to where her father lay tangled in a mass of debris. His eyes were open but sightless.

"No!" Kate cried. It wasn't supposed to end like this for him. Not destroyed by some mindless machine. There had been time. She could have given him CPR. Something. Anything.

She looked up at the hole blasted in the wall. The H-K was gone.

She gathered her father in her arms and held him, her body wracked with sobs. Not like this, she kept repeating to herself.

Connor came over to her. He could see now that she had been hurt in the explosion. Her leg had been cut just above the knee, and she was bleeding. But as far as he could see it was nothing major. Blood was seeping from the wound, not spurting as it would, had an artery or major blood vessel been severed.

He disengaged her grip on her father's body, took her by the shoulders, and tried to pull her away. Gently. The H-Ks would be back. He was sure of it. "There's nothing you can do now," he told her, his tone compassionate. He could write a book on what it felt like to lose someone. "Come on."

"I can't," she said. She looked up at him, pleading, and shook her head. "I can't."

"Yes, you can," Connor insisted.

She tried to turn away, but he pulled her back and

looked into her eyes. Willing her to understand what had to be done. She was covered in blood now, her own and her father's. She was on the verge of collapse.

"Kate, listen to me. He wanted you to come with me. To get to Skynet and shut it down."

She kept shaking her head, as if she could blot out the death and destruction around her. But she allowed Connor to help her to her feet.

She almost collapsed, suddenly feeling the sharp pain in her leg. Connor helped her catch her balance.

She nodded after a moment.

Connor pulled his AK-47 and knapsack from the debris behind the desk. "How much time do we have?"

Terminator was at the door, looking toward the corridor. "Fifty-one minutes," he said.

"We better hurry," Connor told him.

He and Kate followed Terminator through the general's outer office and into the broad corridor as the T-X turned the corner and came directly at them.

Terminator stepped between them and the charging T-X. "Run," he said, and he stepped forward into her charge.

Connor grabbed Kate by the arm, hauled her around the opposite corner, and they headed down the corridor in a dead run.

At the last instant T-X leaped into the air and kicked Terminator in his face with the heel of her boot, putting all of her considerable power into the blow.

It was a force even stronger than the H-K's missile, sending Terminator smashing into the wall.

T-X came down light-footed as a cat, and without a glance at Terminator started after Connor and Kate.

Terminator's CPU was unable to register surprise, or at least not the human variety, but he was able to register a reevaluation of new data that his processor instantly used to overwrite an old subroutine. The T-X model was stronger, much stronger and even more agile than he had been programmed to expect.

He would not make the same error twice.

Before the T-X managed to take three steps, Terminator came off the wall like a prizefighter off the ropes and went after her.

As she reached the corner he caught up, clamping his arms around her upper body, and swung her to the left.

She went with the direction of the force, then dug her shoulder into his chest and slammed him completely through a steel-reinforced concrete wall into the executive staff men's room.

Terminator no longer held confidence that he could win this fight. At the beginning he'd evaluated his chances of disabling the T-X at 18.773 percent. His estimate based on the new data was now at 4.331 percent, with a ± 4 percent margin of error.

But his program allowed for no options other than the preservation of John Connor's and Katherine Brewster's lives.

A sink flew off the wall, shattered porcelain peppering

the stall doors like machine-gun fire. Water gushed from a broken pipe, and a section of the tile flooring cracked and sagged under the pressure of their combined weights landing with such sudden force.

T-X had broken free, and she turned to step back into the corridor, but Terminator grabbed the broken sink by its drain pipe and swung it with all his strength at her head.

Her cranial case nodded under the force of the blow, otherwise she seemed undamaged.

She turned back to Terminator, grabbed him between the legs, lifted his bulk off the floor, and tossed him like a piece of trash across the men's room into the stalls that crumpled like tissue paper.

Even if he had been human, Terminator would have felt little or no pain. As a human his adrenaline would have been coursing through his body. As a cyborg a series of action circuits were firing, providing the electronic equivalent.

He was pumped, as Connor would say.

T-X turned and headed for the door, her sensors reaching out for indications from the T-1s roaming at will through the complex for signs of her primary targets.

Terminator rose easily from the tangled mass of stall doors and partitions and in three quick strides reached the T-X.

He grabbed her shoulders and working with her forward momentum drove her cranial case, face first, into a mirror above a sink, smashing the glass and cracking the wall.

He pulled her head back and smashed it into the reinforced concrete wall again. And again. And again.

Connor and Kate held up at the ground-floor landing in the executive wing emergency stairwell.

They could still hear gunfire somewhere above, but the screams had diminished, as had most of the returning gunfire from the Air Force security people.

The machines were winning as they had been designed to do. The only two questions in Connor's mind were how Terminator was doing against the T-X, and how they were going to get out of here without him.

He looked through the mesh-reinforced glass window in the door. Offices, workshops, and labs opened off the long corridor. The place was all shot up. The T-1s had already been here.

There were bodies on the floor, and all the rooms, especially the labs and workshops, were in shambles.

But there was no sign of the robots.

Connor glanced back the way they had come, half wondering if they shouldn't go back to try to help Terminator.

"What?" Kate asked.

"We can't get out of here without him," Connor said.

Kate had followed his gaze. She knew what he was thinking. "Yes, we can," she told him. "I have a pilot's license."

Connor's left eyebrow rose. He nodded, impressed. "Good to have you around," he said, and he meant it. He was starting to appreciate her strength and resilience. She *was* good to have at his side.

"It should be the next wing from here," he told her. They stepped out into the corridor and raced to the end, where they came to another emergency door with a re-inforced window.

The situation here was the same as in the wing they'd just come through. Offices and labs opening off the main central corridor were in shambles. Bodies lay everywhere, and small fires burned here and there, the haze of smoke thick in the air.

But there were no warrior robots.

The entrance down to the particle accelerator complex was somewhere off this last corridor. Connor and Kate stepped through the door and pulled up short. The stench of shredded human bodies hit their noses at the same time, and they gagged.

Pictures and diagrams and artists' renderings of T-1s and H-Ks and other futuristic weapons systems were framed and hung on the walls in some of the offices and work areas.

"God, it's actually beginning," Connor said. This was the future his mother had worried about. The future she had fought so hard to prevent.

They started down the corridor, passing a big, smoke-filled work area. There were a lot of bodies here, where the fighting and destruction seemed to have been more intense than in other parts of the building. A pool of some flammable liquid had collected in the center of the room and was burning.

Connor took Kate's arm again and had started around the fire when they heard the distinctive whirr of a T-1 moving their way.

Kate pulled back, but Connor bodily hauled her to the floor and scrambled as close to the fire as he could stand without being too badly burned.

The T-1, its hunched back and shoulders nearly reaching the ceiling, came around the corner, its treads crunching over debris and bodies.

It stopped short. A red laser targeting beam swept the room, avoiding the heat source of the fire.

The machine was searching for the heat signatures of still living humans. This unit was evidently part of a mop-up squad. Either that or the T-X had sent it ahead to search for them.

Either way the T-1 presented a deadly menace.

Connor eased closer to the fire, dragging Kate with him.

"No," she whispered urgently in his ear. "It's too hot!"

"The heat will blind it," he explained. "Don't move."

CRS

Smoke started to rise from the sleeve of Connor's jacket.

The heat was nearly impossible to bear, but he willed himself not to move a muscle as the T-1 continued its methodical sweep of the room.

The machine sensed that someone was here; it may have heard them coming through the door. But it was unable to detect their heat signatures because they were so close to the open flames.

Its laser targeting beam swept over their bodies, came back, lingered above their heads for a second, and then began to angle directly at them.

The red targeting beam reflected in Kate's eyes, inches from Connor's. She was frightened, but she seemed resolute now. Something had changed inside of her. He could see it in her eyes, in the way she looked at him, in the way she clung to him, her will to survive fully as strong now as his.

He had the sudden urge to lean forward, just an inch, a half inch, and kiss her mouth. Her lips were slightly parted, and her breath, after all they'd gone through, was still sweet on his face.

The beam played across their heads, then moved away to the left, sweeping up and down like a television raster, painting an infrared picture of the contents of the room, line by line.

The rubber wheels of a small equipment cart had caught fire. Black smoke rose from the hubs. One of the wheels suddenly collapsed, sending the unbalanced table with its test instruments crashing to the floor.

The T-1 swiveled with lightning speed, homing in on the noise and motion, and opened fire with its chainguns, completely destroying the cart.

When it stopped firing the sudden lack of noise was deafening.

The T-1 swiveled again, its targeting beam sweeping the room for further movements or heat sources.

This time it ignored Connor and Kate as already classified nontargets, and after a minute turned away and trundled through the door back toward the R&D wing.

As soon as the robot was gone, Connor rolled away from the fire, and heedless of his burns helped Kate to her feet.

"Okay?" he asked.

She nodded. "You?"

"I'll live," he said, and they skirted the fire and raced down the corridor in the direction of the entrance to the accelerator.

■ ■ ■

Terminator knew he had a double handicap: his model had lesser abilities than the newer T-Xs, and he had only a single remaining hydrogen power cell.

Already he was starting to feel the effects his efforts were having on his power circuits. If he ran down completely it could take an hour or more to regenerate sufficient power to operate. During that time he would be helpless.

The primary cause for concern, however, was his steadily diminishing abilities that were only offset by the double imperatives deeply imprinted in his CPU.

The T-X batted him aside again, but before she could step away, he leaped on her back, wrapping his powerful titanium alloy arms around her neck.

The tile floor and concrete slab beneath them finally gave way, and together they crashed through the crawl space and ceiling of the physical plant equipment room below in a hail of broken tile, shards of glass and porcelain, and showers of water.

The sounds of running machinery, refrigeration units, water pumps, emergency generators, and servo motors for dozens of emergency controls such as fire suppression systems, fire doors, sirens, and lights were very loud.

A row of boilers stood like sentinels down one side of the long room, while a dozen power distribution buses contained in large steel boxes were attached to the opposite wall.

Mazes of pipes and cable runs and microwave guides

crisscrossed the ceiling, an entire section just below the men's room bent out of place or destroyed.

The two cyborgs landed on their feet in the middle of the long corridor between the two rows of machinery. Terminator tightened his hold as he tried to force her cranial case off its mounts.

The lower half of the T-X's face peeled back, liquid metal retreating to expose steel jaws and alloy teeth that were harder than industrial diamonds. Her jaws opened, then clamped onto Terminator's left arm, just above the wrist, the teeth cutting and grinding and crushing their way through his leather jacket, his infiltration duraplast skin, and into his hydraulic and electromechanical systems.

Terminator tightened his grip around her neck, pulling up reserves of power as his action circuits kicked in the last of their electronic adrenaline.

The lower half of the T-X's body swiveled 180 degrees at the hips and she hopped up, clamping her legs around Terminator's torso. Her thighs began to squeeze together with the pressure of a hydraulic press.

The T-X released her grip on Terminator's arm, and spun her head 180 degrees so that her optical sensors were locked in to his.

Terminator staggered a couple of steps backward under her weight. His torso support cage and shielding began to shriek and groan under the relentlessly increasing pressure.

Still Terminator refused to relinquish his steel grip on

her neck, or stop his efforts to wrench her cranial case off its support struts.

The T-X rotated her torso so that her entire body was wrapped around Terminator's in an almost sexual embrace, though neither machine had the slightest capability of considering such a thought.

She lifted her right arm, the skin peeling back from her hand and wrist to expose the plasma transmission head that she had jury-rigged after the fight outside the cemetery.

Terminator released his grip on her neck, grabbed her wrist, and started to bend it away when her plasma weapon fired point-blank at his face.

A large section of his duraplast skin immediately seared away under the intense heat, exposing almost the entire side of his cranial case, which was now pitted and scarred.

The blue glow immediately began to build at the weapon's tip as it rapidly repowered.

One section of Terminator's CPU was refiguring his odds of prevailing, lowering his estimate to less than two percent. His double-imperative program spurred him into throwing the T-X that clung to him to the left, crashing into one of the high-voltage power distribution boxes on the wall.

The T-X did not release the pressure on Terminator's torso, and her plasma weapon continued to charge.

Terminator swung her against the power box a second time, the steel crumpling under the tremendous blows.

He swung her again and again, and on the fourth time

the metal box shorted across the 2200-volt copper bus bar in a shower of white-hot sparks.

Both cyborgs stiffened, their servos going into overload, delicate control circuits shunting to protected areas as the high voltage slammed into their metal skeletons and coursed through their electrical systems.

Terminator leaned against the T-X's body, pressing her against the high-voltage bus, forcing the issue that could, if allowed to continue for a sufficient time, result in the destruction of both their central processors.

Suddenly the T-X broke free, head-butting Terminator under the chin, sending him sprawling backward.

He took two steps, and then fell onto a steel mesh platform that extended over a sump trench beneath the boilers.

Before he could raise up, the T-X was on him, slamming her foot into his cranial case that hung over the edge of the steel platform.

Something snapped in his neck.

The T-X smashed her foot into his head again, dislocating the second and third cranial case support struts.

Terminator was no longer able to raise his head, and many of his servo circuits providing power to his lower extremities were damaged or destroyed. His left arm jerked spasmodically.

T-X studied him for several long seconds, then she bent over his body, her right index finger morphing into a long drill bit, a blue glow surrounding the data transfer probe.

■ ■ ■

The "radiation danger" symbol was attached to the steel door at the end of the long corridor.

"That's it," Connor shouted. It was the entrance to the particle accelerator. "We can follow it out to the runway!"

They had one shot now, just one chance to get out of here, and Connor wasn't going to hang around to make sure that it was the right decision.

At this moment, with or without Terminator, it was their *only* decision.

A window in a row of windows along the corridor suddenly burst inward under the hail of machine-gun fire.

Connor and Kate looked over their shoulders to see an H-K hovering just outside.

They had been detected!

The H-K banked sharply to the left and tracked them up the corridor.

An air-to-ground missile dropped from the H-K's rail and ignited.

Connor dragged Kate to the floor as the missile rocketed through the window, shrieked a few feet over their heads, and blew out the steel security door that led to the particle accelerator.

The H-K spun tightly on its long axis, intending to line up on them again for a second missile shot.

Kate jumped up with a cry, grabbed the AK-47 from Connor, jacked a round into the firing chamber, flipped the safety catch off as she'd watched Terminator do, and opened fire on the approaching Hunter-Killer.

She was completely lost in her rage. Her fiancé had probably been murdered by some remorseless machine.

Her father had been cut down by a machine. And still the monsters came on and on, seemingly without end. Heartless. Soulless. Emotionless.

She kept her finger depressed on the trigger, the heavy buck of the assault rifle shoving her backward almost off her feet.

And then the rifle was out of ammunition, and the H-K seemed to hover in midair for a second, before it exploded in an intense ball of flame, scattering wreckage in every direction, some of the pieces crashing through the windows and clattering down the corridor to land at her feet.

Connor stared openmouthed at her. He'd not seen anything like that since his mother.

She turned to him, her eyes wild, her chest heaving as she tried to catch her breath. She was covered with grease and oil from the floor near the fire, with black smudges of blowback from the AK-47, and with blood.

"What?" she demanded, still hyper.

"Nothing," Connor said, spreading his hands. "You just reminded me of my mom."

He looked beyond her out the windows, but the sky was clear for the moment, as was the corridor behind them. It wouldn't last. It couldn't last.

"Let's go," he said. He took the AK-47 from her, and as they headed for the blasted accelerator entrance door he ejected the spent magazine and clapped in a fresh one from his knapsack. It was his last.

They flew down two flights of stairs to the second subbasement, where they entered the particle accelerator control room. The space was no larger than the living room in an average house, but was crammed with electronic monitoring and control equipment and a dozen computer monitors and keyboards.

A door was open to the accelerator tunnel, through which they could see a blue metal tube, about six feet in diameter, surrounded by mazes of wires and conduits and pipes, gigantic electromagnets every ten or fifteen feet, warning and ID tags everywhere, curving away into the distance.

A large placard was posted over the door.

WARNING: INTENSE MAGNETIC FIELD.

Connor rushed over to one of the control positions, where he laid his rifle on the desk and hurriedly studied the display. He might never have been taught English grammar or history, but some of the weirdos his mother had associated with had been computer geeks. They'd taught him some things.

After a minute he started flipping switches and entering commands into the computer, following the prompts he brought up.

Kate turned her gaze from the stairwell they'd just come down to what Connor was up to. "What are you doing?" she demanded. She wanted to get out of there right now.

"Powering up," Connor replied distractedly. He keyed several more commands and then hit ENTER.

Kate noticed a bank of closed-circuit television monitors on which were displayed several locations within the CRS complex.

T-1s were hunting down the last of the humans, killing them indiscriminately. On other screens there was no movement, only bodies.

But on still another screen the T-X was moving very fast down a corridor. Kate backed up a step.

"Oh, God," she said.

The T-X passed the wreckage of the H-K that Kate had shot down. She was in the corridor just above them.

Connor looked up at the last minute and saw what Kate was seeing. He entered one more command on the computer keyboard, grabbed his gun, and headed for the accelerator tunnel entrance, Kate right behind him.

The big machinery was powering up with a tremendous noise. Super-cooled magnets were being hit with liquid nitrogen, power circuits were coming up, and powerful vacuum pumps were eliminating the air from the accelerator tube itself. It was like being inside someone's insane idea of a factory gone mad.

Over that noise they could hear the T-X in the tunnel behind them.

Connor turned in time to see her less than thirty feet away, her outstretched right hand surrounded in a blue plasma glow.

There was no way that they could outrun her.

No way. He was sure of it.

CRS

Connor and Kate ducked behind one of the outcropping electromagnets as the T-X's plasma weapon fired, the intense blue beam missing them by inches.

The noise in the tunnel was increasing in volume and pitch as the coils around each of the toroidal magnets were cooled by liquid nitrogen. The closer to absolute zero the wiring got, the more electric current it could pass and the stronger the magnetic field became. It was building exponentially now.

Red warning lights began to flash as Connor charged his AK-47 and stepped around the magnet to fire at the oncoming T-X.

A klaxon began to blare, blotting out even the powerful noise of the vacuum pumps and the hum of the magnets.

The T-X was less than twenty feet away. The blue glow at the transmission head of her plasma weapon was so bright it was almost impossible to look at with the naked eye.

Connor lined up on her head and started to pull off

a round when the AK-47 was ripped from his hands. It smashed into one of the electromagnets with a resounding metallic clang and held fast.

Connor looked from the T-X to his weapon. He stepped back a pace. "It's working," he shouted to Kate.

The T-X raised her weapon arm directly at Connor, but it was jerked violently to the left, dragging her to one of the magnets.

She looked at Connor, and then tried to pull her arm free, the metal shell around the accelerator tube distorting under the pressure she was putting on it.

But she was caught fast, and as the magnetic field intensified her entire body was drawn to the tube, stretched out as if she were on some medieval torture rack.

Even the T-X's tremendous power was not sufficient to free her, and as the field continued to build, her features began to distort, her mouth and eyes sliding to impossible angles, her entire body flowing toward the core of the magnet.

Her endoskeleton began to vibrate like a horribly stretched violin string, shrieking and squealing, as the artificial liquid steel that was used to lubricate her mechanical joints was slowly forced through her body and into the center of the magnetic field.

Still, the T-X continued to fight with every gram of her strength, her programming forcing her to continue up to the very point of her own destruction. She had no other option.

Her mouth opened, and as if she were a human being

in pain and anguish at being burned to death at the stake, she emitted a powerful scream.

Kate stepped out from behind the magnet, and stood behind Connor, watching what was happening to the monster.

"Just die," she screeched, not able to take any more. "You bitch!"

Connor lingered for just a moment longer, fascinated by what was happening to the T-X, but then he turned and with Kate raced down the tunnel in search of the way up to the flight line in front of the hangars.

Most of what could be thought of as Terminator's artificial intelligence, his main CPU circuits, were intact. As were ninety-five percent of his subroutines.

But the rest of his functions, mental as well as physical, operated as if he were in a fog. As if he were a human trying to wake up after a particularly deep sleep, or an alcoholic whose functions were impaired.

His motivational programs had been especially affected. Much like a schizophrenic who realizes that what he is experiencing is not real, and yet can do nothing about his fantasies, Terminator understood that he had been altered by the T-X.

But there was nothing he could do about it.

Terminator slowly raised his hands to his cranial case, which he lifted into place on the three support strut ball joints, and snapped them back into place.

Able to sit up now and hold his head upright, he got to his feet where he remained for several moments, his head cocked to one side as if he were trying to figure out where he was, what had happened to him, and what he was supposed to do next.

He didn't feel as if he were under the direct control of the T-X, but he couldn't be certain.

A small hole had been drilled into the temple of his cranial case, and it crackled with blue plasma energy, but he could feel no pain in the human sense, only the dull fog obscuring a portion of his motivational programming.

He headed to the nearest emergency exit, his movements jerky at first but smoothing out as if he was learning all over again how to move and function.

T-X was fully cognizant of all her neural paths. Her body was bound to the electromagnet by a force that by sheer dint of strength she could not break. But she was not unconscious, in the machine sense of being on standby, nor was she without her reasoning powers and her still considerable abilities.

Slowly she was able to morph her plasma weapon back into its containment field, and just as slowly morph the diamond-tipped cutting saw into place.

Her mental acuity was up to speed, but her electro-mechanical functions were sluggish.

The saw came to life with an angry whine, and millimeter by millimeter the blade edged against the wall of the accelerator tube.

At first nothing seemed to happen as the saw made contact, but then a long streak of sparks shot away, and seconds later all the air in the tunnel seemed to be focused in a hurricane-strength gale past T-X's saw hand, and into the breach of the accelerator tube's vacuum chamber.

An impossibly loud whistle rose from the widening gap, and the powerful hum of the electromagnets immediately began to wind down as the entire system went into its automatic shutdown mode.

T-X slid down from the tube, her features beginning to coalesce into their normal shapes, her strength and ability to function returning as the magnetic field rapidly died off.

Something had gone wrong. The accelerator was turning itself off. Somehow the T-X had managed to wreck something.

The placard at the base of the shaft read EMERGENCY EXIT—WARNING AN ALARM WILL SOUND.

Connor pulled down the access ladder, slung the musette bag of explosives and fuses over his shoulder, and started up first. A siren suddenly began blaring in his ears.

There was no telling what they would find when they got to the surface. The diagram he'd studied in General Brewster's office showed that this shaft opened behind one of the hangars across from the west wing of the main R&D building.

They'd seen what the T-1 robots and the H-Ks had done, and it was more than likely that they were still up there searching for live humans to exterminate. He didn't want Kate poking her head up into a maelstrom.

Steel rungs rose up the inside of the shaft. At the top was a steel hatch, with a locking lever.

Connor looked back to make sure Kate was okay. She gave him a reassuring nod, and he slid the latch to the left, freeing the hatch.

Girding himself, he eased the hatch open just enough so that he could see outside. There were wrecked cars and trucks on fire. A couple of helicopters and a military transport were also damaged, and bodies were scattered everywhere.

But nothing moved so far as he could see.

He eased the hatch all the way open, climbed out, and keeping low, scurried the ten feet across to the rear wall of the hangar.

His sudden appearance drew no response. The T-1s and H-Ks were nowhere in sight for the moment.

Kate poked her head up out of the escape shaft and he motioned for her to come ahead. She climbed the rest of the way out and ran over to him.

When they had driven in through the main gate, he thought he remembered seeing several small aircraft and helicopters parked inside this hangar.

"This way," he told Kate. Together they raced along

the back of the hangar to one of the small service doors that Connor eased open.

There were several aircraft inside, light planes and a couple of bigger helicopters. They seemed to be intact, and there were no robots here. From this angle he could better see the burning transport across the flight line and more bodies. The scene looked like a war zone.

Kate lit up. "My dad's plane," she said. "I trained on it."

She led Connor across the hangar to a single engine Cessna 180 with a blue stripe and wheel pants. The civilian registration painted on its fuselage was N3035C.

She checked in the window to make sure the key was in the ignition, and she and Connor pulled the chocks away from the wheels.

Connor looked up as Terminator entered the hangar, and all of a sudden he felt as if they had been delivered. The fight wasn't over, but with Terminator back it was less of a lost cause.

"Yes," Connor said. "He made it." He started over, but something wasn't right. Terminator's movements were stiff and jerky, like a puppet's.

"Get away from me," Terminator said. There was something wrong with his voice too. It was distorted.

Connor stepped back, closer to Kate. Whatever shit was going down now was definitely not right.

"Leave," Terminator warned. "Now!" It seemed as if he were fighting something inside of himself.

"Let's go, John," Kate said.

Connor nodded, but he kept his eye on Terminator as he climbed into the right-hand seat, and Kate got in on the pilot's side. Without thinking they locked their doors.

Kate frantically threw switches, the gyro compass, the radio, VOR and DME, and set the altimeter to what she remembered was the field elevation.

"Come on, come on," Connor urged her to hurry. He pulled the knapsack off and tossed it in the backseat.

Kate turned the key to engage the starter but nothing happened. Nothing was working. She had missed the master switch. "Shit, I forgot to—"

Terminator was at Connor's door. He pulled it open, popping the flimsy lock, and yanked Connor out of the plane, tossing him on the concrete floor.

Connor tried to scramble away from Terminator who was right on top of him. "You can't do this."

"I have no choice," Terminator said, his voice still badly distorted. "The T-X has corrupted my system."

The Cessna's engine came to life suddenly, revved up, and then settled back to a few hundred rpms.

"No! You can't kill a human being," Connor argued, still scrambling backward, trying to get out of Terminator's reach. "You said it yourself."

Kate leaped out of the airplane, ran directly at Terminator, and jumped on his back, tearing at his optical sensors.

"Let him go!" she screeched. "That's an order!"

Terminator threw her aside as easily as batting a fly

off his shoulder, sending her sprawling against a big, rolling tool chest.

He stopped for a moment and looked at his raised hands, almost as if he knew that he had done something bad.

"You can fight it," Connor shouted. "You're fighting it now."

"My CPU is intact. But I cannot control my other functions." Terminator advanced another step toward Connor who continued to back up.

"You don't have to do this. You don't *want* to do this."

"Desire is irrelevant," Terminator said, still advancing. "I am a machine."

"That's not true! You're more than that!"

Terminator grabbed Connor by the jacket and tossed him onto the hood of a Humvee parked just outside the hangar's main doors.

Before Connor could move, Terminator was on him again, grabbing his neck with one hand and drawing the other back into a fist that could crush a man's skull like an eggshell.

"What's your mission?" Connor shouted in desperation.

Terminator's head jerked as if he had received a jolt. "To ensure the survival of John Connor and Katherine Brewster."

"You're about to fail in that mission!"

Terminator's entire body began to tremble. As if fighting a tidal wave force inside of himself, he cocked his fist farther back and drove it down, with every kilo of his force.

CRS

Until this moment Connor never believed that Terminator could hurt him. It was like a child's faith in its father.

He raised a hand to ward off the blow.

At the last moment Terminator diverted his fist to smash the Humvee's hood inches from Connor's head.

"I . . . I cannot," Terminator struggled with the words.

"You know what you have to do," Connor told him. "You know my destiny."

Terminator's entire body shuddered again. His optical sensors glowed with an incredible brightness, blood red, as if they were heading for overload.

It was clear that he was no longer in control of his functions. He was fighting some colossal internal battle. Something had to give way in his system.

"I have to live," Connor said.

Terminator seemed to focus on Connor for a moment, then grabbed him by the jacket and tossed him aside.

Terminator brought his fist down on the hood of the Humvee, caving in the heavy gauge metal like tinfoil.

He threw his head back and uttered a guttural, plaintive otherworldly scream, then stopped, jerked upright, looked at something in the distance, and shut down.

The light in his optical sensors winked out, and Terminator remained frozen in place, unmoving, unblinking, apparently unaware of his surroundings.

Connor got to his feet, a great sadness and weariness coming over him as he stared at the closest thing to a father he had ever known.

Terminator was dead.

There was nothing Connor could do except make sure that he and Kate lived into the future. They owed him and the human resistance that much.

He turned on his heel and sprinted back into the hangar where Kate was struggling to her feet. She was dazed from hitting her head on the tool cart.

"Are you okay?"

Kate looked at him, and then out at the flight line at the motionless Terminator. "What happened?"

"He couldn't do it," Connor told her. "He shut himself down." He gave Kate a critical look. "Can you fly?"

She nodded, and he helped her back to the plane where he handed her up into the pilot's seat, then hurried around to the passenger side and climbed in.

They buckled their seat belts, and Kate checked to make sure that the controls moved freely, that no locks were in place. She eased the big throttle knob forward, the engine responded, and they taxied out onto the ramp.

She had to maneuver around Terminator and the destroyed Humvee as well as burning vehicles and the bodies. Everywhere there seemed to be bodies, civilians as well as Air Force officers and security troops.

The humans hadn't had a chance. LAW rockets might have helped, and perhaps if there'd been time to get the Army National Guard out with a couple of tanks, the fight might have been less one-sided.

But even then Connor doubted if the outcome would have been much different.

Kate turned onto the taxiway that led to the main east–west runway. She automatically dialed up the tower frequency that was posted on the control panel, and reached for the microphone when she realized that there would be no response.

In the distance they could see the control tower was badly damaged, all its observation windows shot out, smoke curling from inside, and no signs of life.

The fight would already be spreading out now in preparation for the nuclear war. A war that no one in their right mind wanted, and a war no one ever expected would be fought this way.

"Are we okay on gas?" Connor asked, to distract her. She was starting to drift because of the unreality of what was happening around them.

She gave a start and glanced at him, and then at the fuel gauge that showed more than three-quarters full. She nodded. "Plenty."

"Then let's get out of here before another one of those flying robots shows up," Connor said.

Kate pulled up at the intersection with the runway, and turned toward the east, into the wind. She checked her controls again, and then holding the brakes ran the engine up to 1850 rpm, held it there for a few moments, then switched to magneto one. The engine dropped about 25 rpm, and came back up when she switched to both. It dropped again, this time almost 50 rpm when she switched to magneto two, and came back when she returned to both.

"Ready?" she asked.

"Anytime," Connor answered.

Kate firewalled the throttle, released the brakes, and the Cessna gathered speed down the runway. At sixty miles per hour, Kate pulled off the carburetor heat and the engine picked up another 150 rpm. At seventy-five she eased back the wheel and they lifted off, building speed for the best rate of climb and then accelerating as she slowly bled off the flaps.

T-X emerged from the particle accelerator emergency shaft and went around to the front of the hangar. In the distance to the east she spotted what looked like a small plane gathering speed and altitude off the end of the runway.

She enhanced her optical circuits, focusing on the light plane. It showed up in her database as a Cessna 180, registration N3035C belonging to Brewster, Robert.

She watched for a full minute longer while the Cessna turned and apparently settled on a heading just east of north.

Her processors brought several options to her head-up display, but Crystal Peak indicated the highest confidence at about ninety-five percent.

If they had acquired the necessary data from General Brewster, there was a chance that the humans, John Connor and Katherine Brewster, could have a major negative impact on Skynet if they were allowed to reach the control center core. This could not be allowed to happen.

T-X strode purposefully into the hangar, passing the inert Terminator without so much as a glance, and headed directly for a Bell Iroquois helicopter parked by itself in the open.

It was not quite as fast as the Cessna 180, but it could take off and land anywhere. It did not have to taxi out to the runway and the time saved would be enough.

Into the Sierra Nevada Mountains

From the air, Connor could see fierce fighting going on over at the main side of Edwards. The carnage was spreading even faster than he had feared it would.

They were running out of time to stop Skynet. Any delay, no matter how slight, would put them over the limit. They would be late, the war would begin, and there would be no turning back from the fight to the death between the machines and the human race.

The future, as Terminator had painted it for them, was a bleak one.

"Okay," Kate said. "Zero-one-five degrees. Fifty-two

miles, our maximum airspeed is about one-sixty."

Connor glanced at his watch. They would touch down at Crystal Peak, if they didn't get lost, in about twenty minutes. Just time enough. "Thirty-two minutes left," he said. He looked at Kate. "It's just you and me now."

She nodded but didn't say anything. After losing her fiancé and her father within the space of one day it was a miracle she wasn't a complete basket case.

Connor got the knapsack from the back, and started arming the one-kilo bricks of C-4 with fuses.

Kate watched him work. "John, what if we can't . . ."

"There's enough C-4 here to take out ten supercomputers," he told her. "We're going to make it, Kate." He looked up into her eyes. She was frightened. He offered her a small smile. "The future is up to us."

She nodded and turned away to watch out the windshield. The Sierra Nevada Mountains rose in front of them, even more bleak and forbidding than the desert beneath them.

"I saw the future," she said.

Connor looked up, startled. "What?"

"I had a vision. A waking nightmare," she said. "There were robots, and explosions and fires." She shivered, and then looked at Connor, wanting him to believe her. "Bodies too. Hundreds, maybe thousands of human bodies, and skeletons and skulls in big piles."

Connor nodded. "I've had the same dream for the last twelve years. Welcome to the club."

"It's true?"

"Not if we can stop it," Connor said. "The future *is* up to us."

She nodded with a new determination, her lips compressed. "Then let's do it right," she said.

CRS

Blackness.

A tiny cursor began to flash in the upper right corner of Terminator's head-up display. The word RESTART appeared.

His diagnostic circuits were the first to come on-line. Starting with his core programs his CPU was tested and rebooted, then brought up to speed one step at a time. But at an increasing rate.

Terminator's optical sensors cleared and began to glow. Animation returned to his features by degrees.

He straightened up, took two steps backward, and then made a complete 360 to scan his immediate surroundings for any dangers.

But the flight line was empty of any live humans or robots.

In the distance to the east he detected the heat signature of a helicopter. In his still not-fully-functional state it took precious seconds to enhance his optics while bringing up a data file.

The machine was a Bell UH-1E/N Iroquois military

helicopter. It was a unit primarily used by U.S. Navy and Marine forces. But he had seen this machine parked in the hangar earlier.

John Connor and Katherine Brewster had left in the general's Cessna 180. The only logical explanation for the pursuing helicopter was the T-X.

Terminator walked into the hangar where a much larger troop transport helicopter was parked. This one, according to his data bank, was a Boeing Vertol CH-46.

It was slow, but it would do.

Crystal Peak

They had been flying for more than twenty minutes and still there was no sign of the installation.

"Maybe we're off course," Connor suggested.

Kate checked her compass and shook her head. "Could be a head wind which would slow us down. I don't know."

"We're running out of time—" Connor said, but then he spotted it, just ahead. There was a long, flat, grassy plateau halfway up a mountain pass. It was protected by what looked like a cyclone fence. A dirt road switching back and forth up the mountain was mostly lost in the trees. "There," he said.

"I see it," Kate said. She pulled the carb heat knob out and backed down on the throttle while keeping the airplane's nose up. Their speed rapidly dropped off and they began to lose altitude as she angled straight toward the end of what at one time might have been a runway.

"Looks deserted," Connor said. He spotted what looked like the entrance to a tunnel bored into the side of the mountain. The dirt road passed through the gates and then straight across to the mouth of the tunnel.

Kate saw it too. "Looks like no one's been here in years."

"That's gotta be it," Connor said.

As they got closer they could see that the top of the mountain above the tunnel entrance bristled with camouflaged antennae and satellite dishes. Whatever was buried in the rock was keeping touch with a lot of satellites and other installations. Probably CRS back at Edwards, and most likely Navajo Mountain, the big Air Force underground facility in Colorado.

They were lined up with the runway. Kate pulled up five degrees of flaps, and then ten and dropped the nose.

The plane wouldn't respond as crisply as it had before because of the thinner mountain air, but the 180 was a beefy airplane with a lot of power to spare in case something went wrong on the first pass.

Connor instinctively tightened his seat belt. He'd never flown much, and as a result he didn't like air travel. Airplane accidents were usually fatal.

Kate pulled up fifteen and then twenty degrees of flaps, and as they crossed low over the fence, she chopped power and held the nose slightly above the horizon.

Connor caught a brief glimpse of a sign posted on the fence that read DANGER—U.S. GOVT. PROPERTY—NO TRESPASSING.

"Hang on, this may be a little rough," Kate warned at the last minute.

Connor braced himself as they set down on what turned out to be an overgrown concrete runway. But Kate's touch on the controls was light, and there was only a slight jolt when the wheels hit. She released all the flaps at once, canceling the last of the plane's lift, and they trundled down the uneven runway.

Connor grabbed the heavy knapsack and even before they had come to a full stop and Kate flipped off the master switch, he was out of his seat belt and had the door unlatched and open.

Kate wheeled the plane into the wind with the last of its forward motion, set the brake, and she too yanked off her seat belt and opened the door.

Connor was right there to help her down, and together they raced across the runway, down a grassy swale, and up the other side to the tunnel entrance.

There were no buildings anywhere within the compound, only the runway, grassy areas, and a lot of boulders and pine trees.

Now that they were on the ground, and seeing the place up close, Connor got the even stronger impression that no one had been here in a very long time.

No *human*, that is.

Just within the overhanging rock lip, the tunnel was closed off by a large, aircraft-hangar-type door with windows above it.

The door was not locked, but its latching mechanism was heavily rusted. It took every ounce of Connor's strength to pull it up and slide it free so that he could open one of the doors on its long neglected hinges.

The floor of the tunnel was concrete with a flood gutter covered by steel grating down the middle. Overhead, the rock was faced with big steel beams that formed curved walls and ceiling much like the inside of a very large Quonset hut.

Lined up in long rows, like so many soldiers ready for an inspection that had never come, were military vehicles—jeeps, trucks, a bulldozer: all painted olive drab, and all old-fashioned, covered with dust and debris that had filtered down from the high ceiling for years.

There was a definite air of neglect and abandonment here. No one had been to this place for a long time.

Connor stopped in his tracks for just a moment. It had been twenty-five years since the first terminator had come back programmed to assassinate his mother so that she would never conceive and bear a son who would one day lead the human resistance.

It was possible that this place had been built as early as that time by the military in anticipation of a coming global thermonuclear conflict.

They were getting ready for Skynet or something like it as long as a quarter century ago.

That would explain the age and neglect that they were seeing here. The place was built for a Judgment Day that had not come.

Yet.

He motioned for Kate to hold up. "Skynet," he said. "There might be more of them."

He pulled out his pistol and fired into the darkness. The shots were shockingly loud here, the bullets ricocheting in the distance like angry bees.

But there was no answering fire. No T-1s coming out of the darkness. No H-Ks hovering just outside the doors.

Connor took the lead into the tunnel, Kate right on his heels, feeling their way around the parked jeeps and trucks when it got too dark to see.

He had no sense that the walls were narrowing, or that the ceiling was getting any lower as they penetrated farther into the mountain. But the air seemed danker, more stagnant. It smelled of rock dust, leaking motor oil, disintegrating rubber tires, and something else. Some distant odor that might have been electrical.

Maybe he was smelling electronic equipment that had been suddenly switched on after lying dormant for many years. It was not a comforting thought.

As best he could estimate they had gone at least one hundred yards into the tunnel when they came to a dead end. A wall made of steel with deep vertical grooves blocked their way.

Connor moved to the right, reaching the edge of the steel wall in five or ten feet, and feeling what he thought was a concrete lip, or edge.

"I think it's some kind of a blast door," he told Kate. He dug in his jacket pocket and found a book of matches. He lit them all at once.

In the sudden glow he could see that he was right. It was a steel blast door set into the concrete, and meant to be raised or lowered into place with powerful electrical motors.

Large air vents, covered by steel bars, opened in the tunnel walls beside the blast doors.

But the entry looked impregnable.

"No way we can blow this open," Connor said, his spirits sinking.

"Maybe we don't have to," Kate said. She'd found what looked like an old-fashioned security station and card reader.

The matches died as Kate slid open a panel that covered a small keypad. A dim light came on that provided just enough illumination for them to see what they were doing.

Connor looked over her shoulder. A small LED screen above the keypad flashed with the single word: STANDBY.

After a moment that word was replaced by the letters and numbers: BLUE 478.

"Now what?" Kate asked. She was just as conscious as he that they were running out of time.

"It's a code prompt," Connor said. He pulled out the red envelope they'd taken from General Brewster's safe back at CRS, and hurriedly flipped through the code cards. He found one tinted in blue, which contained one word and three numbers. "Here. Type in DAKOTA, seven-seven-five."

Kate entered the code and the LED screen flashed: POWER ON.

Lights came to life above the door and in the tunnel ceiling.

The keypad beeped and the LED screen lit up with the next prompt.

"We're almost in," Connor said excitedly.

They could see now that they were in front of a massive blast door. A notice posted to the right warned that this was a SECURE AREA. To the left the notice warned personnel to STAND CLEAR.

Connor was about to look for the proper code card when they both heard the distinctive thump of an approaching helicopter. But close. Behind them at the tunnel entrance.

They turned toward the sound. Now that the lights were on they could see all the way to the end.

A helicopter suddenly crashed through the hangar-type door with a tremendous racket, bursting into the tunnel on a trail of sparks and shooting flames. Pieces of the rotors and the tail section and landing skids flew off in all directions as the machine came to a halt, nose over, in front of a pickup truck.

The pilot's door opened and a woman dressed in a rust-colored outfit climbed out of the machine.

Kate took a step backward, her complexion turning instantly pale. "It's her—"

Crystal Peak

The T-X showing up here was the one thing Connor knew that he should have counted on, but had not.

Kate was losing it. The T-X had become her worst nightmare.

"Come on, come on, the next prompt," Connor shouted at her.

She looked at him. Her mouth worked, but no sounds came out. She remained frozen, but then she blinked as if she were waking from a trance, and turned back to the security screen.

"RED, one-seven-six," she replied.

Connor flipped through the cards, his hands shaking. He dropped them and had to scramble on his hands and knees to pick them up. He found the correct card. "AV-ALON, four-one-two."

Kate punched in the new code. The reader beeped twice, the prompt disappeared from the screen, and was replaced by a single word: AUTHORIZED.

An alarm came to life, and red warning lights began to rotate as a powerful metallic bang reverberated in the thick steel door. It began to rise on the hum of powerful motors.

But it was slow, ungreased metal on metal squealing in protest, a deep rumbling vibration spreading through the tunnel. Small rocks skittered down the walls and dust drifted down from the ceiling.

The T-X was halfway up the tunnel and moving fast. Too fast, Connor gauged. They would never make it through to the other side and get the blast doors closed and locked before she was on them.

They were so damned close.

Connor pushed Kate aside and reached into his knapsack for a brick of C-4 and a fuse. He might be able to buy them some time by setting off a charge as far down the tunnel as he could toss it. If the timing was right he might be able to bring down a section of roof on top of the T-X's head.

If he was off, he could bring the roof down on him and Kate.

A tremendous noise filled the tunnel. It was even louder than the rising blast door. It took Connor just a moment to identify what he was hearing. It was another helicopter, this one much larger than the one the T-X had crashed into the tunnel.

He stepped back another pace.

T-X heard the same deep-throated thump of large rotor blades lifting a heavy machine, and she stopped and turned just as a large troop transport chopper crashed through the already breached tunnel entrance.

This one moved much faster than hers, its rotors

sheared off immediately on the tunnel walls and the fuselage dropped to the concrete floor.

Its weight and momentum carried it over and through the parked trucks, jeeps, and even the bulldozer, all of which exploded like firecrackers on a string.

Still it came, shearing past the Iroquois helicopter and careening down the tunnel like an express train on tracks of fire and sparks.

T-X spun on her heel and headed in a dead run down the tunnel toward where Connor and Kate stood momentarily stunned, rooted in place. The helicopter was right on her back.

Connor came alive first. He grabbed Kate by the arm and propelled her across the tunnel to a maintenance trench in the concrete floor. They leaped into it, and Connor shoved her below the edge, shielding her body with his.

The transport helicopter and vehicles it had picked up smashed into the T-X, engulfing the cyborg in twisted metal and flames. The chopper finally ground to a halt, pieces of burning wreckage flying down the tunnel and hammering off the blast door.

A different siren started to blare, and another set of red and yellow warning lights began to strobe.

Connor and Kate lifted up from the edge of the trench in time to see Terminator emerge from the twisted wreckage of the helicopter.

Half his skin and much of his clothing had been sheared away and burned off in the intense heat of the aviation-gas-fed flames. His metallic endoskeleton was exposed, and even some of his hydraulics and electro-mechanical mechanisms were open to the air.

But he moved like his old self, with a smooth determination. And though much of his duraplast skin was gone or shredded they could recognize his usual sardonic expression.

Connor had never been so glad to see anyone in his life.

Terminator stopped in front of the trench and looked down at them. "I'm back," he said.

The blast door had only opened a couple feet, and then stopped.

Connor and Kate jumped out of the trench as the security keypad and LED screen began beeping. The screen was flashing a new message: ABORT—EMERGENCY CLOSURE.

The blast door started to close with a tremendous squeal. The fire had triggered some emergency circuit. Connor had a feeling that there would be no way to override it.

Terminator brushed past Connor, got down on his hands and knees, and pulled himself under the closing blast door, catching the bottom part of it with his powerful shoulder.

The motors lowering the door hummed in overload, sparks flew from around the edges of the mechanism, and groaning gears stripped with loud cracks as Terminator put his back into the effort to not only hold the massive steel blast door from closing, but to raise it one millimeter at a time.

Behind them, within the twisted, burning wreckage of the transport helicopter, T-X managed to shove an engine block off her chest. She raised her head and torso above the flames, her optical sensors locked on the bottom of the blast door.

Her infiltration covering was completely gone now, leaving only her battle chassis that itself was scarred and dented from the tremendous heat and forces it had endured over the past twenty-four hours.

But T-X's imperatives were still intact, her programs were still up and running, and her prime directive was still driving her actions.

She had been sent to eliminate twenty-two targets. John Connor and Katherine Brewster were at the top of the list.

They were here.

She would kill them.

Terminator's internal mechanisms were strained to their limits, exceeding even their built-in safety and redundancy engineering.

He knew that he would not be able to hold out much longer.

He was also aware that the T-X was struggling to free itself from the wreckage. There was no time left.

"Go!" he told Connor and Kate. "Now!"

The fire and smoke were getting thick in the tunnel, making it difficult to see, let alone breathe.

Connor tossed the heavy knapsack filled with C-4 under the blast door, sliding it all the way through to the other side.

He helped Kate crawl under the door. She paused long enough to give Terminator a grateful look, and then scrambled the rest of the way through.

Connor got down on his stomach and pulled himself under the massive blast door that vibrated like a live beast just above his head.

Terminator's body trembled with exertion. Connor could hear overloaded hydraulics and servo motors, and smell the stench of burnt electronic circuitry. A joint in Terminator's shoulder failed with a loud pop, and hydraulic fluid began to spurt from beneath the mechanism.

"Thank you," Connor said. He had lost this friend once before. It was very hard to go through it again. So much had happened, so much had gone on.

"We'll meet again," Terminator said with as much emotion as was possible for a cyborg.

Connor scrambled the rest of the way under the door, which, at the base, was nearly two meters thick.

Kate was there. She reached down for him when

something clamped over his left ankle, tearing into his flesh.

The pain was impossible to bear, and he screamed.

The T-X, her legs sheared off in the wreckage, held on to Connor's ankle with her right hand and began to inexorably draw him back under the blast door.

Terminator grabbed her wrist with one hand and her throat with the other in an effort to drag her away from Connor.

In the effort his shoulder turned away from the blast door that then inched downward, pinning him and the T-X like a hydraulic press.

The buzz saw morphed from the T-X's left hand, and she drove it into Terminator's chest, just above his one remaining power cell.

Terminator tightened his grip on her wrist, bending hydraulic joints out of position, causing her finally to lose her grip on Connor's ankle.

The door was pinning their torsos even more tightly now. Nevertheless the T-X managed to bring the saw up from Terminator's chest, into his neck, and then into his chin and cranial case.

Circuits shorted out and massive dumps of random data no longer under the control of subroutines cascaded like shivers through his CPU and servos.

Still he did not release his grip, although with what little RAM was left in his cognitive circuits he finally reduced his chances of success to zero percent.

His body, broader at the shoulders and in the chest than the T-X's, was being crushed by the lowering blast door.

He could feel all of his systems going off-line, one by one. And there was nothing he could do to stop his own destruction.

He brought up John Connor's image, now and in the future, superimposed over the images of Katherine Brewster now and then. They were not machines. They were humans, creatures his original programmers had meant for him to eliminate.

But a montage of pictures of interactions with Connor and with Katherine Brewster rippled across his dying memory circuits.

One final course of action was left open to him. The only logical choice.

He released his grip on the T-X, and for a second their optical sensors locked together.

The T-X withdrew the saw and started to crawl the rest of the way under the blast door.

Terminator pulled aside the armor plating in his chest to expose his last hydrogen fuel cell. Without hesitation he yanked the cell out of his chest, trailing wires and mechanical parts, sparks and fluids flying in all directions.

With his free hand he grabbed the T-X by a piece of tubing protruding from her hip and dragged her back.

She turned and fixed him with a baleful gaze.

"You are terminated," he told her.

Terminator crushed the fuel cell to rupture it, and thrust it into the T-X's mouth, driving it deep into her throat.

"Eat me," Terminator said, and the fuel cell erupted with a tremendous explosion.

The Refuge

Kate had to help Connor hobble down an unfinished concrete corridor to a short set of stairs. They had just started down when a wall of flame shot out from under the steel blast door.

They managed to get to the bottom of the stairs and race down the lower corridor when the shock wave hit them with a blast of incredibly hot air, sending them reeling and stumbling forward as if propelled by unseen hands.

The blast door settled on its track with a tremendous metallic bang that instantly cut off the flames and shock wave.

Connor and Kate pulled up short and turned to look back. Connor half hoped to see Terminator appear at the head of the stairs. But he knew in his heart of hearts that would not happen.

He and Kate exchanged a glance and then headed the rest of the way down the tunnel that was lit at intervals by caged lights.

Dust lay everywhere. No one had come this way for

a very long time. A quarter century, Connor supposed.

The corridor ended at an elevator cage. Functional. Industrial. Meant to move people and machines to and from a subterranean control center.

Or was that right?

Connor looked back again for a moment. All the vehicles in the tunnel were very old. Coated with dust. Everything was disintegrating with time. This place was dead. Unused.

According to his watch, they had eight minutes before Judgment Day began.

They boarded the elevator and started down.

Connor opened the knapsack and inserted a detonator into a brick of soft plastic explosive. He was out of breath and operating on his last reserves. The wound in his leg throbbed, and the pain in his half-crushed ankle was excruciating. He couldn't remember when he'd had a decent meal and a good night's sleep. In a bed. Between clean sheets.

He looked at Kate, who watched him with a dubious expression on her smudged face.

"I'll set this for five minutes," he told her. "That should give us enough time to make it back up here."

She nodded. Left unsaid was what would become of them afterward. It was possible that the blast door would never open and they would be trapped down here.

Connor crimped the fuse to start the acid timer and looked at his watch. The countdown started now.

Moments later, the elevator reached the bottom,

which Connor estimated had to be at least one hundred meters beneath the tunnel.

It was dark down here. The only sounds were the noise of the elevator machinery and a distant hum somewhere.

Connor pulled the door open, and he and Kate stepped out, not knowing what to expect.

Lights began to flicker on as old, automatic circuitry activated with their arrival. Classical music, low and soothing, began to play. And they could feel the gentle rush of clean air from ventilators.

Connor stopped short as he began to see where they had come out. They were in a very large, lavishly appointed space, perhaps the lobby of a luxury hotel of twenty or thirty years ago. But brand new. Never been used.

Comfortable looking, overstuffed chairs, long plush couches, and massive coffee tables and end tables were grouped here and there. A fully stocked bar ran along one wall, shelves of books on others.

The ceiling was very high. Parts of the room had been partitioned by frosted glass dividers and doors. Sections of raw rock were exposed as if the designer had used the natural look of a cave hollowed out of a mountain rather than completely disguise it.

But there were no supercomputers here. No command and control center. No sign of Skynet.

"What is this?" Connor muttered, half under his breath.

He limped across the lobby to a large door, which he threw open. Inside was an enormous pantry filled with row upon row of metal shelving stacked with bottled water, freeze-dried foods, canned goods, cooking oils and spices, paper towels and napkins.

At one end of the storage area, racks of grow lights were mounted over rows of hydroponic trays meant to cultivate vegetables and herbs and other plants.

Kate opened another door, which led into a dormitory. Rows of bunk beds and lockers, enough to accommodate at least fifty people, were ready for use.

They were running out of time. The detonator fuse continued its countdown.

Connor hurried past Kate to a third door that revealed a different kind of facility entirely.

This was Crystal Peak's Control and Command Center, and yet it was all wrong. What looked like a waiting area furnished with chairs and couches faced a glass-enclosed computer center raised a couple of steps above the main floor.

The great seal of the United States of America was mounted high on one wall, and across from it, what appeared to be a small television studio had been set up in a corner. Lights hung from a massive, circular concrete slab suspended from the ceiling brightly illuminated a podium that was flanked by the U.S. flag and a blue flag that Connor didn't recognize. Television cameras were trained on the podium behind which was a blue curtain for a backdrop.

Connor and Kate took a couple of steps closer. At the

center of the backdrop, directly behind the podium, was the seal of the President of the United States.

The president was meant to be here. To broadcast his message to a nation that was at war.

Global thermonuclear war.

It was becoming clear to Connor, finally. He sprinted across to the computer center, which consisted of several rows of monitor stations above which were clocks showing the local times at various capitals around the world. But the equipment was old. Twenty years or more out of date.

"These are just ordinary computers," Connor said with growing understanding.

He looked around, frantically searching for something, anything to prove him wrong.

"This isn't Skynet," he said. "There's nothing here. It's just a fallout shelter for VIPs. Only they never got the warning."

He swept a computer monitor off the desk and it smashed onto the floor, its old fashioned CRT tube imploding.

"Goddammit, there's nothing here!" He looked at Kate and nodded beyond her to the lobby and the elevator that had brought them down from the tunnel. "Why did he send us down here to—?"

"To live," Kate said softly. "It was his mission."

Connor shook his head and lowered his eyes. He was spent. It was all over. "There was never any stopping it," he said. The detonator fuse was counting down. Less than one minute to go.

Kate was looking at him, her eyes filling with tears. She had lost everything that she ever valued in her life. "John," she started. "We could just—" But she couldn't say it. Couldn't suggest that they do nothing, remain right here until the C-4 exploded.

One of the communications consoles suddenly came to life, red lights flashing, the overhead speakers crackling with static. Voices, dozens maybe even hundreds of them, jammed the one channel. It was hard to make out at first; there were so many of them. Some of them spoke foreign languages, some heavily accented English. But all of them were frantic; that much was clear.

"Hello, hello. This is Montana Civil Defense. Somebody please come in—"

"Can you read me? This is U.S. STRATCOM. We're at a hardened facility, under attack. Repeat, we are under attack."

"—rumors about launch sequences, command and control have broken down out here—"

It was over. Judgment Day had arrived. Connor looked at Kate, and he could see that she understood that they were too late. That they'd never had a chance.

"Is there anybody there?" a distant voice pleaded. "Is there anybody there?"

Connor pulled the detonator from the brick of C-4 and tossed it aside. Two seconds later, the fuse sizzled momentarily and then popped.

Connor went over to the communications console, studied the controls for a few seconds, and then flipped a switch and picked up the microphone. "This is John Connor at Crystal Peak."

"Connor, what the hell is happening? Who's in charge there?"

He hesitated. "I guess I am," Connor said after a beat.

Kate came to his side and took his hand in hers. He turned to look into her pretty face, into her eyes, into her soul.

Maybe some things have to happen, he thought.

He knew what was happening now on the surface. Hundreds, maybe even thousands of missile contrails would be crisscrossing the evening sky.

By the time Skynet became self-aware, it had spread into millions of computer servers across the planet. It could not be shut down.

Thermonuclear explosions would be erupting all over the world. City busters, the multi-megaton weapons were called. Designed to kill millions of people with one searing blast.

The attack began at six-eighteen P.M. Just as he said it would. Judgment Day.

From the viewpoint of satellites in orbit, this was the time when the earth had no night darkness.

The day the human race was nearly destroyed by the weapons they'd built to protect themselves.

To the west toward Los Angeles and the California coast, bomb after bomb detonated, sending massive nuclear shock waves across the mountains, toppling trees and setting them alight as if they were matchsticks.

I should have realized. The Terminator knew. He tried to tell us. But I didn't want to hear it. Our destiny was never to stop Judgment Day. It was merely to survive it—together.

Above, in the tunnel, a wind began to howl, fanning the dying flames from the wreckage of the helicopters, sending desert sand under the blast doors to scour the burnt remains of the two terminators.

There are others like us. We will find them. And join together. Take back our world.

Terminator's skull was crushed almost beyond recognition. Wires and hydraulics and processor chips were exposed.

But there was still a faint red glow in one eye.

Maybe the future has been written. I don't know. All I know is what the Terminator taught me. Never stop fighting. And I never will.

A tiny electric circuit in Terminator's skull shorted out.

The battle has just begun, Connor thought.

The wind in the tunnel was very strong now and radioactive with early fallout. But Terminator was no longer aware of anything. The faint glow in its eye died.

ABOUT THE AUTHOR

David Hagberg is a former Air Force cryptographer who has traveled extensively in Europe, the Arctic, and the Caribbean and has spoken at CIA functions. He has published more than thirty novels of suspense, including *High Flight, Joshua's Hammer,* and *The Kill Zone.* He makes his home in Florida.